Tracks Thi

Stories Told on the Philly El Trains

By John A. McCabe

Tracks Through Our Lives:
Stories Told on the Philly El Trains

By John A. McCabe

WCP
Pearl S. Buck Writing Center Press
Perkasie, PA

ISBN: 978-1096214830

John McCabe ©
400 Grandview Avenue
Feasterville, PA 19053
(215) 357-9449
undertrees2@aol.com
www.mccabeauthor.com

Dedication

*Dedicated to my Brothers and Sisters
and the Girl from G Street,
and all the guys and girls
banded together by
the street gang we loved
while growing up
in Philadelphia.*

Acknowledgements

A salute to the Pearl S. Buck Writing Center and their staff of learned volunteers at the Writing Center Press who devote themselves to the international legacy and fame of Pearl S. Buck, Pulitzer Prize winning author and Nobel Prize for Literature recipient. Many authors, both novice and seasoned writers, owe them all a debt of gratitude.

First among them is the unselfish, gifted editor of this collection Dr. Anne K. Kaler, Professor Emerita of Gwynedd Mercy University. Her patience and wise counsel helped shape this collection.

I thank Cindy Louden, Director of the Writing Center, for her valued encouragement and support.

I appreciate the expert formatting of Linda Donaldson in the graphic design and layout of this book.

And, of course, I thank my fellow Writers Guild members for their critiques and suggestions.

Lastly, I am indebted to my talented granddaughter Dana Cai McCabe who provided the lovely oil painting used on the cover of this book. Dana is currently an Art Therapy major at Arcadia University. She was born in China and adopted through the former adoption agency at Pearl S. Buck International.

And thus, the Pearl S. Buck influence comes full circle.

Introduction

Climb the concrete stairs and ride the Philadelphia El Train with me to Center City and back – let's see, hear and feel the stories reverberate along the Tracks Through Our Lives.

Some would call this a novel or a collection of short stories told in the form of a novel. Others would say it is a semi-autobiographical adventure and romance.

Tonight, I start seeing us when we were just boys and girls in the neighborhood. In the vision, it is that time in our lives where everything we knew, combined with all that was around us – all that was somehow beyond anything we imagined.

Back then we were the real figures sitting or standing and swaying in the rhythm of those El Trains. So many stories were shared and lived both within and out there, far away from the windows of the trains.

It would be a mistake, however, to call any of it fiction. The guys on da't corner in Philly would tell you that, "Danny Fisher ain't no fiction."

Table of Contents

Prologue

Under Mellow Yellow Streetlights

We got lots of trouble going on with things around us now and tonight, I guess, because I kind of slipped off to the side of it all, I started seeing us when we were boys in the neighborhood. In the vision it was night time and we were running and I thought about how real our dark figures were in the scene. We were real then – not now. Now we are not real. We are less than real now because we are already leaving this place. Then we were the real figures and in the real place and we were time itself. Now time has fallen back a few paces from where we are and we aren't totally a part of it anymore.

Back then, running through the neighborhood and, at that time, we were very, very real. It is like having a body that sweats and pulses compared to one that only fills space. Do you get what I see and what I am looking back at in the dark, maybe on a summer night, somewhere on those streets under a streetlight's electric glow?

Streetlights were assigned the wonder of making moving shadows. Streetlights were for dream walking to enhance the dark, strong shapes of our reality. Only the youthful possessors of our beings could run through those mellow yellow lights over those streets and sidewalks with our darting humanity. We were the figures of hosts of our time as real boys and girls in a permanent flash of the fascinating reality, cast like motion pictures on the walls of our minds.

In Philly before we were born, a streetlight was a gaslight ignited by the lamplighter walking the neighborhood in the early evening. For us in our time, all that gas lighting had been remarkably replaced by electricity, hard-wired on telephone poles we called telly-poles through-out the city. Adequate illumination, as the mandate read, was mounted by city electrical workers on the telephone poles found usually both in the middle of every block and at street corners on thousands of streets and in every neighborhood in Philadelphia. In our childhood place on the north end, the streetlight, still called a lamp by our seniors, was in the middle of the block across the street from our old three-story clapboard home. Its light meant a lot to us and, in our unspoken gratitude, we felt safe as we played endless street games under that yellow, golden glow.

13

We nailed a basketball hoop so it was suspended on the wooden telly-pole and shot baskets day and night. We lived with its comfort and relished its guidance in the dark. We felt safe in the light and worried in the dark between streetlights. And like some ancient, instinctual need, it was home-base for lots of games: we played Red Rover – Hide n Seek – Capture the Flag – and day games with its wires, like Wire Ball. No need of a White Paper or scholarly essay to convince us it was the light of human life. The only time we truly considered its worth was when storms came and blew it out, leaving us in the emptiness of darkness.

As we grew up and as we began to roam the neighborhood, we discovered other streetlights and they became a grid, an extension of what ours was to us, like when you visit your cousins and aunts and uncles. You could count on all of them and we did. I am over seventy now and last night I wandered back to it all and sitting on a curb I was thinking out loud, a habit that developed recently. You find that you are beginning to wrap things up when in your seventies. You hear the sounds of commentary about life coming from your own mind.

Talking out loud was nearly an unconscious behavior but, when I caught myself in the act, I wanted to silence my voice and usually did after finishing a sentence, sometimes two. The streetlight I was sitting under was the one half-way down the block from the corner, which my old gang, boys and girls, used as a teenage hang-out. We even gathered on that corner later in life until everybody moved away or became assimilated into the city population.

What I heard myself saying was, "If we had any idea where we would go and what we would end up doing in our lives back then in that street gang, we would have been in total shock." I tried to stop talking out loud but continued with, "God, guys fought in foreign wars, some died young, some, like Chad who was a gypsy just seemed to disappear another impossibility, some like me had strange things happen to them, Jacque Porter grew out of his own skin and Danny Kurr went to jail for the rest of his life. And Tony Pallato spent decades trying to invent a new source of free energy for the whole world from his gyros – maybe he did and was never discovered before he fell off a motorcycle."

Not talking aloud anymore I thought, "Just a bunch of kids who I used to see under this same streetlight heading for the corner where we were all brothers." Yeah, I could see how you looked up and recognized someone by his or her walk or mere silhouette in that mellow yellow street light. The corner was dark at night, one of the few, and that was by choice so nobody could be sure what we were up to. You sat on the curb in the dark or leaned against one of the old American elms that grew on that street. The streetlight was where you were always indentified and it glowed like stage lighting on featured characters, "Hey," somebody would say and I caught myself talking out loud again, "Here comes Eddy Drake," "Is that so and so," "Who are those guys?" or maybe, "Look at her tonight, she is looking too cool, wow!" And I grew silent again and saw the past appearing like a dream.

We are there, it was a night under that light back then when nights were filled with adventures, running from the cops, meeting up with neighborhood girls, being happy, laughing at the fun stuff and just being you, young and strong and secure in our own world.

We were right under that streetlight in the winter, we were all turning fifteen, and the light enabled those of us who got away to do a roll call as each of us became recognizable emerging from the dark. City streets without lighting are very dark and they can be scary places. There are all kinds of people in the city and lots of dogs to bite you. Criminals were lurking about those places at times. Yet on streets illuminated adequately a safe sense prevails.

That night, when we took a sort of muster call, it was because of what happened after a whole week of collecting discarded Christmas trees, all very dry and brittle. Jimmy Ganner kept an accurate count, Jimmy counted everything with an accountant's accuracy, he announced a total of 217 while Benny Maher and Chris Farrell threw the last few trees on top of the huge pile in the middle of an abandoned lot. Wingnut, the one among us whose ears were the most prominent, held a roll of burning newspaper in his right hand like a torch bearer and a cigarette lighter in the other. After Wingnut had all the hair on his head and eyebrows and arms singed, the blazing tree inferno leaped into the night sky like something nuclear.

Just before the Philadelphia Fire Department arrived or maybe as the first fire fighters were making their way to the lot, nearly 30 guys all about fifteen ran off in whatever direction they happened to be facing. Some ran between nearby houses, some dodged traffic down the streets, others flipped up a familiar manhole cover and went down into the sewer, one behind the other.

The police were soon walking around the blazing trees but not one of the thirty volunteer arsonists was anywhere visible in that vicinity. No matter where the escapees darted off to they would all eventually make their way back to the corner but only as fast as their individual sense of safe timing convinced them to do so.

The place under the streetlight, there adjacent to their corner hang-out, was where a gathering assembly of the totally assured believers boasted gleefully of the greatest Christmas tree, unlawful bonfire in the history of the neighborhood.

When Wingnut walked out of the darkness and was warmly acknowledged by the others, reeking of the distinct smell of burnt human hair and all that was left on his head kinked in twirls of charred curls, he was heralded as true hero of the season, it was that streetlight that was both stage and safe place again for the boys of fifteen. With about ten girls neatly dressed in winter coats, scarves, mittens and hats in their midst, even the cops would mistake them for innocents.

At sixteen, adventure became more dramatic and cars got stolen and raced. Staging boarding the stolen cars happened just beyond the streetlight as something done in the dark. Crime itself was always left to lurk beyond illumination. On the corner, those who would not steal or ride in hot cars peered cautiously and at a distance through the safe zone of the light into the shadows trying to identify the thieves and their accomplices. All larceny matters of any concern were given blow-by-blow verbal description by those roosting on the corner, "Big D's got that black Impala again." And someone would announce more details, "Yeah, that's him and Bear and Cub are in the car, see?" and another voice saying, "You can see 'em from here, man!"

The stolen car, another borrowed Chevy with Phillip Brown at the wheel, would spin wheels as it left and the streetlight would wash its glow of innocence over the scene and those sitting all the while on the corner were safe again with no worries about the cops coming or excuses for the larcenist among them. Phillip Brown, whom we called Brownie, would be driving that night's trouble. Two cars with loud mufflers and radios blaring parked under the light, welcomed by all who hung there. As Jake Herley's three-window Ford coupe, and Mickey Rodger's forty-nine Merc convertible glided in, the corner's space expanded under the streetlight and teens walked out there and all around the two Hot Rods. Sandy Wendler started to jitterbug with Nora Clemens. Their shadows from the streetlight played against the wall of a row of garages across the street as figures of the dance of the drama of youth.

At seventeen, we had beer, and the streetlight glistened in the brown glass bottles of cold quarts of Iron City beer. Nick The Stick's Buick with 8" radio speakers provided the Rock-n-Roll and "Since I Don't' Have You" inspired Danny Fisher and Bridget Moore began to slow dance over that very center of the streetlight's shining where a more

16

delineated circle of light was cast earthward. Another gang from the Southend of the city, called South Philly, showed up just then and the fight over Flossy Bender ensued. A guy that the South Philly guys called Little Caesar, who was not little, groped Flossy and took a cigarette right out of her mouth and started smoking it. When Clare Hood tried to give Little Cesar a push and he pushed back, Crazy Harry and Bear and Nails and Big D and Spots Daniels started circling the South Philly boys and more than twenty guys off the corner came out to the lit area. Bridget Moore and Danny Fisher kept dancing as the crescendos of "Since I Don't Have You" inflated the sense of prowess for the combatants.

Soon shadows flickered over the street paving and up and down the curbs. Light that was previously gentle and mellow yellow began to flash between agitated bodies and flaying arms and fists. Little Caesar collapsing to the street snuffed out his own shadow gripping his head he was down. The South Philadelphians running kept yelling threats until they disappeared in the darkness.

Nearly beyond the range of the streetlight Nick the Stick's Buick took a fist blow on the hood from the retreating Cesar and contours of the dent pooled reflections for the mellow yellow light that once again filled the space out there beyond the corner. Fats Domino was crooning about "Blue Berry Hill," while my memory shifted ahead in time.

At eighteen, the world under the streetlight began to change scenes and life also began to take the street residents from their perches on the corner to other callings and gradually smaller and smaller attendance was seen and the light gave itself to less and less. Armies and Navies were gathering older boys and schools beyond high school and real jobs took over those corner times which were given all too briefly to city kids in Philadelphia.

When I was seventy, Clare Hood called me (now she was Clare Dole). We nicknamed her Clare Blair because, when she first started dating Dole, she wanted to change her name from Clare to Blair. She had a fancy streak.

Clare-Blair told me Boots McGrath's wife Lillian Donatone had died and where her death viewing was going to be held. I knew I had to go. The funeral parlor was in the old neighborhood on Oxford in what used to be called The Sketchley Mansion, not a mansion really, just a big white house near the trolley stop.

I felt strange waiting in a block long line to see Lillian's body and not knowing anybody in the line but one of the old gang, Billy Green we called Greeny, or back then he got called Rubber Legs the Dancer.

17

Legs was good company but I would end up alone afterwards. Lillian looked like somebody's great grandmother and she was. They had pictures of her from back when we knew her. She was a beautiful young girl with a shape that made you want to look. When it was over and unbeknownst to Rubber Legs, I walked into the neighborhood by myself. I walked to the old corner and gazed for minutes at the area under the streetlight, the paved street, the sidewalks, the grass along the curbs and the one American elm still growing there that may have been there when we were kids. The streetlight wasn't the same. It was a new type and shed a different kind of light but it did so in the same place. So it worked for me and a parade of memories began to capture me.

I was old, however, and alone and it seemed surely that no one hung on that corner anymore, no one that is except everyone I remembered suddenly, and they were everywhere. Those minutes projected my friends all around me like a cinematic work of Elia Kazan and me standing in the lit up area. I could see where our old light cast its center brightest and I could hear the cars with Hollywood loud mufflers and dual exhausts and multiple carburetion feeding full-race engines.

I remembered the laughter and all the voices, each voice mystically that of only one person in the world, one of them whom we loved even if we didn't know at the time that we loved them. I could hear the Rock-n-Roll from the car radios or a Phillies' game broadcast from Mr. Dockstader's porch a few doors up the street on any summer night and I saw one of the girls dancing under the streetlight. She was Jewish and Jules Dockstader's old girlfriend and she was doing the Twist with Mandy Cerone.

Just when I must have seen them all, they all disappeared and there in front of me were my brothers and sisters and the kids on my block under our streetlight playing in the mellow yellow light and Billy Hendrikson was yelling, "Red Rover, Red Rover, Time for Joey McGrath to Come Over!" and I almost darted at seventy across the street, but instead I turned away and walked out of the light. But the light had a way of staying with me and, as I walked, I was never aware of it being darker.

=/=/=/=/=/=

Years later when I started climbing the stairs to the El station every day, with its cage-like steel fencing and three concrete landings to break the sixty-foot climb, I would look back over the city. Philadelphia was always busy, but busier than ever, with industry and train tracks and factories. The sounds were incessant, coming from the truck traffic to and from Tioga Terminal, or the big avenues, Cottman, Frankford,

Allegheny, Girard, and Lehigh, and Market Street. Nevertheless, in all that noise, my memories and my childhood jumped out at me in the unforgettable voices of the past.

Those voices were now my history. Below me, I could see far out over our old residential streets. All the stories started there, some with endings, some never finished, and most would never be ended or begun quite the same, depending on who was telling them.

When I climbed the steel stairs to the station platform, I wondered if anybody would be around that I knew. Would they be waiting like me, or for me to arrive? Who would I know or recognize, and would I talk to them? It was an everyday curiosity, and it really centered on wondering who might talk to me?

No one, talk to no one, was the rule; no one would want to talk? It wasn't cool, it wasn't done. People who had to talk to somebody, or to nobody, were given little attention or cautiously ignored.

In those days, those times when the El ride was more than transportation, more than going or getting someplace – it was more like a daily space held in time, and a place in itself. I wanted to talk to the special ones: the girl from G Street, the teacher I had at North, and the guy with the Temple hat who helped me push a drunk off onto that next station one day – that soused trouble-maker with a fist like a club who wanted to knock somebody on the head.

I never knew the Temple guy's name, but he got greeted daily nevertheless. I did the rules of the ride. I never really conversed with anybody, nobody except Danny Fisher. Danny Fisher, like me was an inner city kid who later became a newspaper man in Philadelphia. He wrote human interest stories for a living. I have been a high school history teacher ever since Danny and I graduated from the University.

I met Danny Fisher again when we were a little older. It was one of those days when, as always, I was watching the blind guy, and being nervous about him, knowing we were nearing his stop. I was so impressed by how he could always figure out when his station was coming up. Once again his stop was coming. He had the great dog with him, but the dog never moved until the blind guy started to get up. I knew he was going to miss his stop, he was asleep. The dog would stay on the floor. I got happy with myself, happy that I was going to wake him up in time.

I was a quiet guy, and not bold enough to wake somebody up for his stop, even a sleepy blind guy, but I was going to do it. It was not being un-cool, not this. He was sound asleep, and the station was getting

19

close. I always wanted to be brave like that and do the right thing, when somebody had to act. I'm sure Danny Fisher and I touched one of the guy's arms at the same time. Danny came from the swaying crowd of strap hangers at the other end of the El train car. I hadn't seen Danny Fisher since our days at University.

Danny and I watched the blind guy and his great dog stepping off the train and walking across the station at Lehigh Avenue as if dog and man were a single life form, an inseparable team of two needy beings joined at the heart. It was there and then, that commuter rail user's morning, that Danny Fisher and I reconnected, and as old friends would say of us, we started talking for the rest of our lives.

Here are some of the stories...

Bridge & Pratt

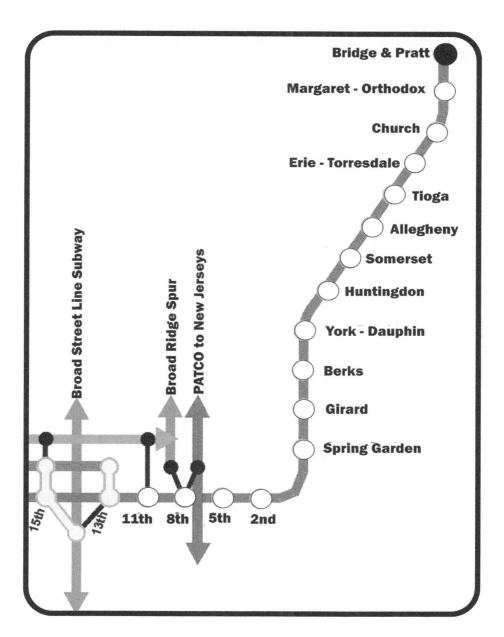

Bridge & Pratt

Margaret - Orthodox

Church

Erie - Torresdale

Tioga

Allegheny

Somerset

Huntingdon

York - Dauphin

Berks

Girard

Spring Garden

Broad Street Line Subway

Broad Ridge Spur

PATCO to New Jerseys

15th

13th

11th

8th

5th

2nd

Chapter 1

Danny and I were waiting to board the El at Bridge and Pratt, when he asked me if I had ever expected to go to the University when I was a kid.

I said, "If I'd let the nuns influence me, I'd have thought I was the village idiot. They had me pretty much convinced that I was a spineless jellyfish, and a bold brazen article, and a moron."

Danny Fisher said that he was given that same inferiority challenge when he was in first grade, but he beat the rap by sheer defiance. Then he said, "Bridget Moore talked me into trying to get accepted to the university after I got out of the army."

I said, "How long have you known Bridget?"

"I think she was in my playpen." Then laughing, he said, "Since grade school, man."

Thinking of what he said, I asked, "You're talking first grade, man. What can you still remember about first grade? Are you kidding, first grade?"

"Yeah, first grade and I remember."

The Cleansing

Catholic School Days

It was Ricky O' Brian and Boots McGrath and me, Jeremiah Hopper, walking the cobblestones between the trolley tracks on Oxford Avenue. Boots was placing rocks on the tracks and Ricky kicking them off almost as fast as Boots put them down. When I looked back over the city block we just came from, you could see one stone still on the tracks. We got scared and stopped in the middle of Oxford and Rising Sun Avenue to watch a trolley ride over the rock.

Boots was biting his knuckles all the while but the speeding trolley never stopped or swerved and was soon discharging passengers, right in front of us. Four nuns stepped off with Doctor Bennett talking to them and Gus the plumber, carrying their shopping cart.

Boots said, "You dumb ass, O'Brian. If you hadn't kicked off the rocks, they would have rid the world of four of the meanest nuns in Holy Innocents."

"Good afternoon, Sisters," I said respectfully hoping they didn't hear Boots or O'Brian's reply when he said, "Only three of em are Nazis, McGrath. The little one is nice to everybody."

"Have a nice day, Sisters," Boots said.

One of the nuns was staring him down. I knew she had to make him look away or, for the complete defeat, have him look down. It was an animal instinct and what even zoo captives will do sometimes when you lock in eye-to-eye contact with them. Boots would know, at his age that, if she didn't defeat his eyes and young male mind set, she would retaliate in school the next week until his spirit was soundly defeated.

She was one of those combatant nuns with a porous-looking bulb for a nose, no real face, just puffy mounds of pink, scrubbed flesh surrounding her featureless, ink-blue eyes and her starched wrapped headdress. Boots looked down, spitting on the ground and shuffling one foot on the concrete. I thought the spitting was a good balance, but dangerous.

The four nuns obviously aware of a partial victory walked off after Doctor Bennett handed one of them a small folded paper. We continued on the cobblestones, the trolley moving right in front of us, sounding like a siren with its steel wheels on steel rails, rolling, in its crushing noise.

Boots got out cigarettes and we all started smoking and spitting at the poster of a Philadelphia politician tacked onto a telephone pole. It was comfortable in the city air in September but the iron tracks reflecting the white sunlight looked like streaks of molten steel as they did at the time of their extruded birth in the hot end of some old mill. It caused us to squint and then leave the tracks for Palmetto, a side street in the neighborhood.

"What's the little nun's name?" I asked.

"Sister Mary Delicatessen," said O'Brian.

"Yeah, Jeremiah," said Boots. "But they don't need names. They all go by the name, Stir, They're like the Screws, those prison guards in the movies are called."

"No, it's Bernadette, Bernie," added O'Brien. "I heard 'em call her, Sister Bernie."

"How come she's nice?" I asked.

"Cause she's young," said Boots reflectively. "Wait till she busts a few skulls," he added. "She's actually pretty now, so she's gotta get ugly first, then the old nuns will train her good. They practice those ruler and clicker-stick cranial blows in the back basement of the convent."

"Hey, Boots, that one nun was eyeballing you, man. You're gonna be put in the grinder this week," said O'Brien.

I instantly remembered Sister Marie Baptiste's claims to put bad kids in her sausage grinder when we were in first grade. We were walking towards Monk's cigar store where we sat on the steps until it got dark and we had to go home finally as the weekend dissipated under streetlights and because of school the next day. Today was Sunday, the day we always ended up walking the streets and sitting at Monk's until it got dark.

=/=/=/=/=/=

It was a rainy Monday morning. We were being cooled by the gusty breezes rushing into the open top windows on the church side of our classroom. On the other side, the two oak-grained doors to the hall-way were left open and the somber silence they invited stayed out in the dimly lit passageway with its high-arched ceiling and paneled walls. The young priest was coming that day.

The classroom's long row of large wooden sash windows gave view to the church. The church had narrow elongated windows like those on the towers of castles. It was a medieval look and I often thought of

24

chains and blood and dungeons when I stared at it too long. The church was old grey stone with a shiny black tiled roof. It had a misplaced look as if it had existed in another age and time. In stormy weather the church seemed like a heavy cloud, a rock-walled chamber where rain and lightning were always expected. I don't think the building ever evoked a thought of God, just some kind of ancient buried power and shadowed silence.

As I sat in the classroom staring at one of the elongated windows, the thought of blood, dark blood-stained earthen floors, came to mind. It was not a deliberate thought but a spontaneous one that materialized as it often did in one form or another when I looked at that stone church in a daydream state.

I had seen McGrath's nose bleed on the first day of class when Sister Robert swung her suitcase like book bag off the end of her desk and hit Mc Grath on the side of his head banging his nose onto a desk. Then the nun hit Boots twice because he spilled ink on the girl beside him, Bridget Moore. We all called her "Much Moore" because she had bigger breasts than the other girls. Boots had just bent down to prevent Bridget's uniform from contacting the ink he had spilled on her desk while his blood squirted from his nose and filed his mouth repeatedly.

When Bridget saw McGrath's blood, she stood up clutching the side of her legs and said, "It's okay, Sister, I spilled ink on this last year."

"Sit down, Miss Moore! Aren't you the Gutter Snipe now defending the likes of McGrath."

"I think he is hurt bad, Sister."

"Hold your head back, Mc Grath! Pinch your nose tight." She held her own deformed bulb of a nose as an example. "Hold it! As for you, girl , you will sit down and be quiet in my class. We all know you think of yourself as a fashion plate." Sister's eyes always crossed rapidly back and forth horizontally when she yelled.

I think it was Boots McGrath's blood I saw while looking at the old church. At least I think so. In any case it was a strange and unsettling thought for me. I decided to keep my eyes away from those windows and that side of the room. It was getting close to 10:00 AM, the time the priest was supposed to come. A nervous mood penetrated the classroom. Sister Robert was unusually inactive and students were straightening up their things and assuming noticeably erect postures.

Ricky O' Brian stood up in the back row and said, "Stir, a mouse just ran from the cloakroom right behind you and out into the hallway! Stir."

25

Sister Robert looking back over her shoulder said, "Go tell Mr. Dungan. O'Brian. Find Mr. Dungan!".

O'Brian went out the rear door of the classroom and reappeared in the front doorway with a cigarette in his mouth. He motioned to Boots McGrath in the first row for a match. Boots threw his cigarette lighter at O'Brian with Sister Robert seeing none of it. She was standing rigidly before the cloakroom door, her back against the class. O'Brian left with a short wave to a new boy. Seconds later he was back in the doorway with a cigarette sticking straight out of each ear and one still in his mouth. He vanished in another second. Somewhere down the hallway, O'Brian shouted, "There's more mice in the stairwell, Stir!" We heard the outside doors open and close amidst the muffled laughter all around us.

A priest, this time Father Connelly, visited the classroom six times a year, in the beginning of the year, as he was today, and the four report card visits and then at the end of the year. Father Kevin Connelly was only two years out of the seminary. At each of his visits, he would attempt to teach some aspect of religion and then ask questions. Some of the girls in the class always talked about how cute he was and some of the boys may have imagined him to be competition.

He entered the classroom at 10:05 without knocking and sat at Sister Robert's desk while she awkwardly sat herself on the old kitchen chair in the right front corner of the room. She took a pill out of a prescription bottle and swallowed it. The kitchen chair was usually used to seat the latest person being punished. Her behavior with the priest in the room was so subdued that she all but disappeared in motionless silence, her posture bowed. Both her folded hands and her face pointed toward the floor.

"Who knows the meaning of the Latin words, "Kyrie elieson"?

No one answered until the silence brought more tension in to the room and Sister Robert's foot began to slide back and forth on the floor. Richard Trotter, honor student and altar-boy, raised his hand breaking the tension with the correct answer. The priest stood up and frowning said, "Are you learning anything that would cause any of you to love God?" Leaning back on Sister Robert's desk, he accidentally knocked over her statue of Saint Michael stabbing Satan with a broad sword. The statue fell loud onto the floor and broke apart.

With a sudden cessation of the cool outdoor breezes, the odors of the lunches in the cloakroom captured the classroom space. It was a putrid smell coupled with the constant odor of the Pine-sol cleaning fluid used in every part of the school. Sister Robert was quick to lift the

26

broken pieces of the statue in her both hands as if cradling an infant and just as fast to cast burning glances toward the priest, now clearly her unwelcome intruder.

Distracted, I almost turned my eyes to the old church but I was caught in an imagined picture of the priest standing in the front of the class with Sister's Robert's punishment ball in his mouth. I imagined him, his eyes frantic with pain, struggling with nostril breathing and the image of myself one morning when she caught me talking and passing notes to Geraldine Devlin. I had to hold the air-filled rubber punishment ball in my wide-open mouth all morning and again after lunch that day.

The priest bent down picking up a piece of the statue Sister Robert hadn't seen. She cut her hand taking it from him. With that I turned away and staring at the old medieval-looking church, I saw her with a grip on his youthful black hair, pounding his head against the blackboard the way she did to the kids when she was totally provoked. Usually somebody had to touch her to get that treatment and they would invariably be doing that while talking back to her outrageous charges. The old church building hadn't failed me. I had the most gruesome images to deal with in my mind. I was seeing deep red, almost purple blood, like that which came from Boots' mouth and nose.

Sister Robert put the broken statue into a shopping bag and sat down again on the kitchen punishment chair. Bridget Moore raised her hand knowing she would not be refused with the priest present and asked aloud, "May I go to the girls' room, Sister?" Years later she told me she had her period that day and was trying to find a way to care for herself before it was too late to avoid embarrassment. She heard about what happened when she left and always asked me about it. We were friends for years after grade school.

She left the classroom and walked down the hall and outside across the schoolyard to the always cold cemented floor bathroom where by sitting down on the open toilets you automatically set the flushing mechanisms triggered when you stood back up. I listened to her whisper to one of the other girls when she returned that Mr. Dungan nearly caught her and O'Brian smoking behind the bathrooms. I heard her and, of course, for me it was another vision of corporal punishments.

The priest remained standing, and as if checking to see if the nun would really be simply sitting there again, he looked at her for a long moment and then went over by the big wooden sash row of windows with the church roof behind him. He said, "Sorry about the statue sister, I will get you a new one."

While Bridget was still whispering, O'Brian came back to the class out of breath. The priest had to let him by before he continued. Looking at us all he said, "Let me repeat my question, is there any part of your education and the time you spend in class causing you to love God?"

Mr. Dungan appeared at the door also breathing heavily.

"Excuse me … sorry, Father. Sister, dem mice ain't gonna hurt ya. As quick as I am, and seems I do catch em" He looked directly at O'Brian, "I can only catch those rascals at night. But I'll catch the divels, by God," said Mr. Dungan as he disappeared into the hallway.

The priest walked to the door Mr. Dungan had used. He leaned out and looked down the hallway and said, "And now for the third time, is there any part of your education and the time you spend in class causing you to love God?" After asking his question, he stood studying Sister Robert for another moment and then looked around for any hands. I was shocked to see Boots had his hand up.

"Go ahead, son. What have you to say?"

"What answer would you have given when you were our age, Father?"

I became nervous for Boots as Sister Robert stared at him. It was then that I realized her nostril openings were black and large, like cavern entrances to her dark interiors.

The priest, his clean-shaven chin rising up, while one hand sent fingers spread into that youthful black hair, smiled saying, "Well, answer a question with a question. Good question. What's your name?"

"Everybody calls me Boots, Father, but it's McGrath, Bartholomew McGrath."

"Okay, Boots. I haven't thought about this in a long time, but when I was in first grade my mother worked seven days a week and my father drank seven days a week. I was neglected, and that was the easy part. But I was never bathed regularly and I used to innocently play with the dirt caked on the outside of my heel below my socks and on my forearms and behind my ears…"

He had the immediate and complete attention of all of us in the classroom including Sister Robert. You could hear every entering brush of the outside breezes, which had returned to the schoolroom driving out the sickening smell of the rotting lunches and the foulness of Pine-sol.

"My first grade teacher, Sister Marie Baptiste, grabbed me by the tie and was, all of a sudden, shoving me down the hall. All the doors to the other classrooms were closed. It frightened me because I never saw the doors all closed before. I thought that all the other kids and teachers left the school, all but me and that angry nun."

"Sister Marie Baptiste was very tall and thin and it took an effort on her part to bend down to my size for the shoving. I was crying halfway down the hall but determined to be brave, so I could face my brothers and sisters when they found out I had been bad in school…"

Sister Robert got up and walked to the front door of the classroom. When Sister Robert disappeared into the hallway, leaving the kitchen punishment chair sitting empty as if it was her representative until the young priest sat on it.

Boots sat down awkwardly, as if to listen to the priest. He was wise enough, however, to sit down and remove any more attention to himself.

The priest took his hand out of his pocket and pointed unconsciously to the door Sister Robert had just exited and then pointing to where she had been standing said, "Sister Marie Baptiste took me to the seventh grade classroom, my sister's grade. Inside the room I was made to stand facing the entire class. I quickly looked for my sister Ann, but with so many faces, I didn't find her until they called her name out and she stood up.

My first grade nun told my sister's teacher how dirty I was. My sister's teacher yelled at me about how she would lock me in the convent cellar if I came to school dirty again, Then she made my sister go in the cloakroom and get a bucket of dirty water that the janitor left there and using the janitor's old gray rag, soaking wet with the stench of Pine-Sol and vomit, she was ordered to wash my face and arms and my neck while the whole class looked at me…"

"Now what happened when I was your age to make me love God? Well, it was my sister Ann, at your age that gave me a reason to love God. She took my shame on herself and comforted me and, when it made her cry, she cried for me because I was too dumb or innocent to know how cruel it all was. But Ann took it all on and she always seemed to love God and pictures of horses and my drunken dad and the kids in school, and so I did too. In other words, a bad place, and some bad people created a need in me. They also created a way to see and know God when he was around. Ann, and the Christ in her, is probably the reason I am a priest."

Boots began to stand up again but, looking toward the door for Sister Robert, he only partially stood. Holding his desk with both hands, he asked the priest, "Hey, Father, you gonna send Sister Robert away someplace?"

The young priest, with a look as if he just swallowed Sister Robert's punishment ball said apologetically, "That's up to the pastor, Boots." Then looking at youthful faces around him, he stood up and said, "Look, kids, I don't know what got into me, I never told that story to anybody. Keep it between us. Okay?"

=/=/=/=/=/=

Boots and I and Geraldine Devlin and Bridget Moore walked the cobblestones between the trolley tracks that afternoon and Boots said, "I think half the nuns we got snuck out of the women's wing of the SS when the Second World War ended. What a religion, ya gotta be nuts to call this jazz Christian."

"Except for that priest," I said. "He ain't too bad at it."

"Shit, Hopper, he isn't doing diddle-shit about the beatings and all. And those nuns, the crazy ones, will be right back here next year," cried Boots.

Bridget Moore grabbed Boots' hand and walked him off to the place where the trolley stop bench sat off the turn on Oxford Avenue where they could do some kissing.

Geraldine Devlin and I wished we were doing the same so we went to the woods up past the block beyond Monk's Cigar shop and we kissed each other until there was no world except our own.

After he told me the story, I asked him if Bridget helped him with his career, because what I remembered about her was that she was a good student, smart and always first in the class,

"Are you kidding, man. I think if the paper knew how much she helped and edited my work, they'd fire me and hire Bridget."

"That's nice," I said,

"Here," he said, opening his briefcase, "I got something she just sent me from down the Jersey Shore. She was there last week."

"You mean something she wrote?"

"Yeah, wait a minute, we got time...,' Danny said, thumbing carefully through his briefcase.

He took out a folded paper that looked like a letter written on a greeting card and handed it to me. The El train was coming to a noisy stop at Margaret and Orthodox Station.

I started to read. She had a title at the top of the page and I became engrossed and quite surprised:

Two on the Railing

It was surprising to look over at the woman talking to me near the beach at Cape May, New Jersey. She was an enormous lady with wild blowing hair and a set of green/blue eyes that seemed to own the seashore, matching the rolling waves and low skies over the surf.

At first I didn't want to pay attention to her but her voice was more than a match for my indifference. The first words heard clearly were, "The autumn has its stillness, that hushed calm."

I said, "Sorry, what did you say?"

As if she didn't hear me, she kept talking, nearly whispering actually. She was leaning on the same railing, so she needn't talk loud.

"It also brings its sounds; winds bringing sweeping intrusions, that rapping on our windows. We know time as a swift current, deceivingly slow when watched all day, but a rapid ghost no less. We are all fast travelers, our flights move against the cosmic grandeur, and tragedies of the universe."

I was smoking and she looked at my cigarette with regret. I said, "Go on, please, what were you saying?"

"Well, we are also what we were, and magnificent in it all. I was young like you, dear... tall, stunning. What's your name?"

"Bridget."

"That's my name!"

"Oh, gheez, that's remarkable. You enjoy the autumn... Bridget?"

"Yes, I come here every year, Bridget... to watch the migrants, the birds."

"Always Cape May?"

"Yes, dear, and you?

"The same, 'Wings in Odyssey,' the pamphlet says, 'Visitors in magnetic navigation.'"

"Do you think about how their worlds are filled with waiting, calling out to the wind, voices from mysterious eternities?"

"I should."

The big woman, like a bird on a rail, rose up and waved goodbye. I never saw her again.

Margaret - Orthodox

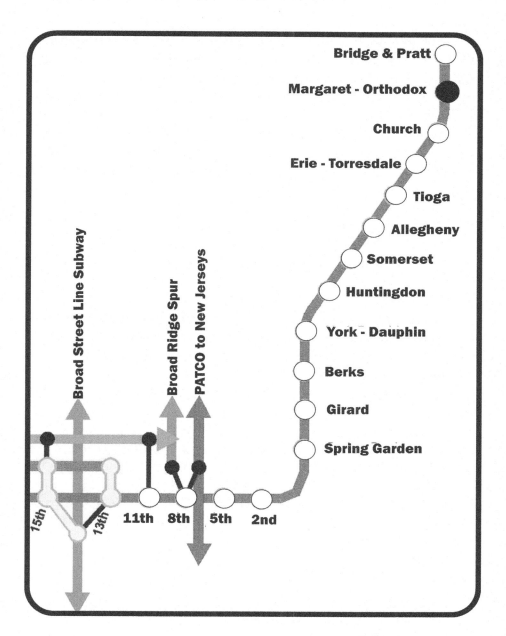

Bridge & Pratt

Margaret - Orthodox

Church

Erie - Torresdale

Tioga

Allegheny

Somerset

Huntingdon

York - Dauphin

Berks

Girard

Spring Garden

Broad Street Line Subway

Broad Ridge Spur

PATCO to New Jerseys

15th

13th

11th

8th

5th

2nd

Chapter 2

I didn't see Danny again until it was almost summer. In Philadelphia that meant heat and humidity. Danny was standing off in the shaded station area. He was dressed in jeans and sneaks and not like a working stiff, like the rest of us in the commuter class. He somehow stayed cool looking on that sweltering August day.

"Hey where ya been?" I said, adding, "You off today?"

"Don't have the job anymore," he said.

That was the time when Danny was changing the Rags, as he called the newspapers.

"You quit?"

"Yeah, ya gotta do that now and then..."

"What happened?"

"You mean the day I left? You mean you wanna know how, or why?"

"Well, yeah."

"I'll tell you. The paper became a mule for carrying one-sided politics. One day I felt like I was stuck under somebody's front porch. Remember how we hid under the porches when we were kids?

"Not me, but, yeah."

"Well, what would you do if you felt like that, crammed up in the dark?"

"I'd get out."

"Yeah, sure, but it's important to really feel like you got out, ya gotta walk it off..."

"How'd you accomplish that, Danny?"

"Walking, I walked it off."

"How's that?"

The Bridge Walker

Well, you see nobody ever walks across the Pratt Bridge, the one down by the airport.

I felt like one of those twisted characters in a Film Noir. I had my dark suit, brown but not black. As I crossed the highest point over the river in South Philadelphia, I was wondering if the latticed steel footing would really stay in place.

In my mind, the way I saw myself in the film, I looked like a jumper, some guy about to splash the river. I guess that's why one of the bosses came for me. They could see me from the building. I might have walked all the way across Philadelphia but the guy felt he had to pick me up. So I told him I wanted a ride to the trains up at 30th Street Station. From that point, he would feel he did enough and leave me alone.

Maybe I'd walk the tracks when he was gone. Nobody ever walked the tracks anymore, not the way we did when we were all kids. God, it has all changed. When I got there, the old train was just as appealing as the tracks. I got in the train walking from car to car until I felt like sitting. I did and put my feet up in great comfort looking out the window at the things that passed.

Me in my dark suit, in my mind, crossing the Pratt Bridge like a Film Noir guy speaking to myself in that laconic style. I was that guy trying to get his mind untwisted from all the scenes of his life, scenes that never really made sense, things you did all your life for some reason like you were supposed to.

What a time! I thought. Unexpected, I had one of my Walden Pond moments. Maybe Thoreau had the best idea after all but I was far from Walden Pond this day. The bad economy had a real sense of mystery though… Thoreau just wasn't a Film Noir guy never could be. Not like me on the bridge. He'd have to drown somebody in Walden Pond. The Bosses were Noir guys.

Finally the train ride got too long and I wanted to walk again. I got off at a wrong station two stations before my stop and walked to Bridget's apartment in the dark alone. When I got there, Bridget had a platter in the oven for me. I told her about the Pratt and one of the bosses taking me to the train.

She touched my shoulder and asked me if I wanted some apple-sauce and if the Pratt had a sidewalk and, looking in my eyes, she asked, "Did the walk help?" She always understands. She lives in scenes which Film Noir or Thoreau never discovered or looked for. I wondered why she never seemed ordinary and how any of us connect with what we need. I pushed away the thoughts of the jobless stuff while Bridget went about her kitchen barefoot.

Bridget would never walk the Pratt, but she knew I had to.

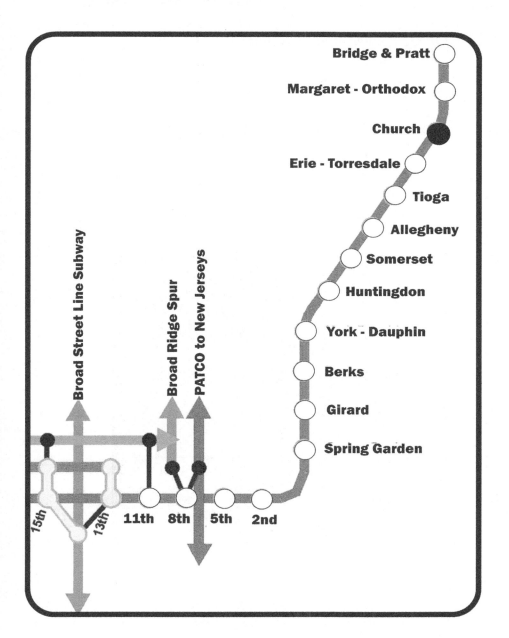

Bridge & Pratt

Margaret - Orthodox

Church

Erie - Torresdale

Tioga

Allegheny

Somerset

Huntingdon

York - Dauphin

Berks

Girard

Spring Garden

Broad Street Line Subway

Broad Ridge Spur

PATCO to New Jerseys

15th

13th

11th

8th

5th

2nd

Chapter 3

This is a story Danny had published in a Philadelphia Magazine. I read it on the El as soon as he handed it to me. He was telling me about fights he was in at the Cambria.

You can see the Cambria Boxing Club from the El, and, ever since the "Rocky" film, we Philly guys are proud of our boxing history. I fought a real boxer, a Bantam Weight Champ, in a barracks fight one time so I was very interested.

This is Danny Fisher's Story about a Boxer and a kid from around the Church Street Station.

Tom Dempsey & His Midday Tiger

**A John McCabe story short-listed in a
County Cork Ireland writer's contest.**

When you get old, so old that you can comb what's left of your hair with your towel, you don't always realize that you are old.

That is the way now for Tom Dempsey. Time goes by differently for him, however, not just the predictable shifts from morning to midday and then to night, but more than those. Time takes rests like old women walking up a steep hill, or what white-haired men do leaning on their canes to turn and change direction, moving only hands and elbows first and all so slowly, as if they had all day and all the rest of their days.

It's all different somehow, maybe in the in-betweens more so. Take, for example, the minutes before first light or when a particularly quiet afternoon wanders off to the edge of evening. That's a time once unnoticed but now it is different than before. The one that strikes like a tiger is that of noontime when the sun is directly overhead. That is where old people get pivoted by time. Like being a living hour-glass, they feel the inversion and even the sense of hesitation of the solar path at its zenith; the old at this time fall into yet more ageing each day when the day clock strikes that noon hour.

It is like hearing heavy wooden doors open and close far off in a distant room in a big house. If it all continues, and it does, the days fold over and on to the eternal. The young are unaware of the commotion as well as the silence of it all. There are no doors opening or closing to the young. All days are one upon another. Importance to youth is only in the now.

For some reason Tom finally gave up on being young or trying to convince anyone that he ever was young. When you enter the days of young and old being the same, and not being either, you are old and it is all one element of time, your time. Then you see the crossing-over thing up ahead, itself a time to live and to live no more. It beckons you and maybe some of your friends have already crossed.

In a dreamy way, living old is not unlike boys and girls balanced on a fallen log trying to get over a flowing stream. People like Tom brave the crossing one after another until all have crossed. Tom Dempsey, almost that old, but still just this side of it, asked himself, "Will we ever get to pause a bit?"

For Tom Dempsey, the noon hour and the sun directly overhead, was something quite opposite of peace and pause. Tom once confessed, "You realize it was all supposed to encourage you to do your best. You measure every moment and whether it was good or not good. The time is yours until you carry it across that log for the last crossing." He thought again of the Gypsy kid and how it was for the two of them, and what happened. That is always when that midday tiger leaps.

=/=/=/=/=/=

Tom Dempsey was over six feet and nearly two hundred pounds in his prime. He had wide shoulders and long legs, and he was narrow at the hips. Tom was a Huckster, a peddler of produce, and a Philadelphian. He worked out of an always clean-and-green, city delivery box truck, with a ramp and a hand cart and a wooden wheelbarrow on board. He sold fresh fruits and vegetables in the city of Philadelphia under the El Train where it turned at Bridge and Pratt Streets. He was there every weekday except Mondays and he only worked half the day on Saturdays, and never on Sunday.

Tom had a boy work with him every summer, and in the sixties, there was one boy he would never forget. It was a kid named Chad Smith, a gypsy-looking kid, neither White nor Black or Asian or Hispanic. Chad Smith did the entire wheelbarrow and hand cart hauling while Tom always set the heavy ramp in place and put it away at the end of the day. Tom also set up their presentations, the displays, as fastidious about displays and produce as he was about how clean the lime green truck was kept. He wore simple clothing, jeans and one color shirts and brown shoes. What stood out on Tom was the hat. He had a flat brimmed straw, and though he was totally a city guy, the hat was Amish style, or definitely farmer. The hat wasn't without soiled spots. No, it looked like a huckster's hat.

Chad Smith never looked like he cared about clothing at all, but he did. He always had Wrangler blue jeans on and his shirts were pullover T's with a pocket and sleeves. He had good arm and shoulder muscles and his very agile feet were sneakered in black Keds only. All his clothing was worn, and the sneaks more so, but he always looked clean, even when perspiring in Philadelphia's humidity. When all was unloaded and set up, the kid would climb in Tom's wheelbarrow with a green pillow kept in the cab of the truck, and once comfortable, would sit there watching Tom sell and deal with the people.

He liked Tom's way with them, his genuine smiles and Tom's admiration for the produce. Tom told Chad many times, "Hey, kid, greedy industrialist and so-called engineers and scallywag merchants make and sell their junk and contraptions to unsuspecting buyers, while we sell what God makes since he does the coloring and the shaping and the goodness of our products. If the customer's got a gripe, he needs to take it up with the Big Boss."

And when he said such things to Chad, speaking right to him that way, the way Tom always paid respect to people, the gypsy in the kid showed itself as he listened in the sheer beauty of the kid's thoughtful eyes. He had headlights, as Tom called the boy's eyes that would melt a person. His eyes were contemplative, total peace. They were humble brown with whites that gave them highlighting like new snow, and his lashes were long and black-black and they seemed to glisten. Tom would tell his friends "Not for nothing, but the kid attracts the ladies and girls. I see that stuff when their making their purchases," Tom was, in his own way, a handsome man, strong and weathered well, but the kid was charm. His sitting in the wheel barrow never hurt business.

On the hottest of summer days, they set up two full-size beach umbrellas, which they also used on days with light rain. Tom had a portable Philco Radio that broadcast day games from Veterans Stadium or sometimes, what no one expected – Italian opera. Tom loved Italian opera. He said, "If the woman listening knew what those men were saying to them, they'd swoon for the guy." He said, "Only the Italian guys sing to their woman that way, it's beautiful." Then he would add sarcastically, "Only the Italian woman could deal with em when they weren't singing, is what I'm telling ya . . ."

When the Italians weren't on it was a Philly D.J. Joe Niagara on radio station W.I.B.G., and the Rock and Roll you could hear surrounding Tom and the Boy. There wasn't much else to enjoy around Bridge and Pratt. The elevated trains were loud and the people on the sidewalks and crossing the streets were all in a big hurry all the time.

If you noticed anything else, it may have been the pillars of sunbeams coming down from the openings in the metal structures holding up the elevated subway cars that screeched up from downtown Philadelphia every so many minutes. Tom was always aware of what that sunlight did for his displays. On cloudy days, he missed the lighting and maybe the work was dulled by the weather, but Tom's Irish liked the rain as well. He had a folding chair to place under one of the umbrellas for such days when a few customers would still come because the rain was light. He smoked a pipe when rain drizzled but never any other time, not around the produce.

Tom and the boy almost never stopped talking to each other during the days. They always had so much to talk about. Of course they clammed up for those customers who demanded their attention or submissiveness but, other than that, the dialogue was ongoing and easy, Philadelphian, and shared freely even with the passers-by in earshot.

Their days started very early, before daylight, at the busy docks at the Food Center in South Philadelphia. While most all the other hucksters and small store owners and all of the big outfits had electric pallet jacks and forklifts to ride on and collect their produce procurements from those cash-only Food Center vendors, only Tom and the boy and a few chefs had no such thing. Tom was the only one still using a wooden wheelbarrow. To Tom, any kind of forklift was an avoidable expense and not compatible with the delicacy and purpose of their edibles. It was to a Dempsey, a hands-on business, as it was to Tom's father and his father. The Irish, even in America, have a reverence for the produce and for dirt farming and its place on the earth.

Tom and Chad almost never stopped talking to each other whether at Bridge and Pratt or in the truck or those early mornings on the docks at the Food Center. At the docks they were in a community, like row home living in the city where everyone knew everybody and lots of them knew everybody's business, or thought they did. Walking up and down the place looking for the best produce prices, they spoke or nodded to nearly the whole population of the place using only first names and nicknames. Nicknames were very widely used and memorable creations. The Kid was called "The Thumb" because he only had one good thumb. He lost part of the other thumb trying to get a carton of grapes while standing on the forks of a narrow aisle lift truck in Penza's cooler. He was hanging onto the fork lift mast up in the drive-in racking when his thumb got caught. Mr. Penza cried for the Kid when that happened.

Tom was Tom; no need for a nickname when your real name was friendly enough or too easy to say to be changed. There were exceptions of course, like Albert Alanzio not being called Al or Lanzo, or something other than the two words nickname "Santa Claus, but he had a beard, and it was a six-inch-long totally white beard. Al Alanzio also had a shape like a guy who ate a lot of food. Thus the Santa thing was a nickname for life but, peculiar to nicknames, Ralphy Alanzio was always called "Santa Claus's Brother," no matter that Ralphy was really Albert's cousin. That was all part of Food Center life in South

Philly. Once in a while a nickname got dropped or forgotten, not very often, it was rare but it happened to Tom. When Tom was younger in his twenties, when the Food Center was still up on Dock Street off the Delaware River, Tom had a reputation of being the Irishman nobody wanted to be socked by, because he was strong and wiry and had a hit like Rocky Balboa. He went for the eyes with every punch. Tommy was a good boxer, a club fighter at the Cambria Athletic Club up on Clearfield Street in Kensington near the Frankford El. His father made him stop the boxing but Tom kept the fisticuffs in his spirit, just in case. Anyway, the nickname that went away was "Tiger Tommy."

Every trip to the Food Center took Tommy and the Kid a couple of those early morning hours while the city slept. Those hours of finding and selecting their fruits and veggies, always included two coffees at Norm's restaurant in the middle of it all. The best produce for their quick turnover business was the most ripened. Ripe fruit was more attractive, and both ripe fruit and vegetables wholesaled for less because the Food Center merchants had to get rid of it or shove it off the edge of the docks for the city trash truck's pick up every late afternoon. Shelf life was money, or it was all just rotten apples.

Tommy knew exactly when to buy each commodity, talking prices down while short stepping backwards, or in side-to-side steps all the while he bartered, but only if one of the Merchants got his attention. When a price got interesting, he was on the balls of his feet. When he began to work clockwise around the seller, leading with the left side of his body where his wallet would get patted sporadically by his fist, the keenest of the merchants knew the moves. Prices, nevertheless, got lower because none of the merchant vendors could be sure if Tommy was faking them out.

That was what was going on way back when Tommy was a savvy kid in his twenties. It was around then that Tommy clocked a guy over some bad peaches, which was how he got into the boxing to begin with. He KO'd the Manager of the Food Center's cousin, Eddy the Duke Cerone, when the peaches he sent up to Tommy's dad were all white mold and brown with rot and he wouldn't make good on them. Later Tommy was taught to do body damage when in the ring, but he started and ended most fights going for guy's eyes. If he hit a nose coinciden-tally fine, but he wanted to hit you on the eye. Tommy shut both of Duke's eyes in four consecutive jabs to end the fight with an unseen right cross. Duke was the retired Bantam Weight Champion until "Tiger Tommy" put his lights out. Then he was nothing as a boxer. One guy

43

tried to start a new nickname, "Peaches," for the Duke, but he regretted it; bantam weights are quick.

As Tommy's boxing manager, Blinky Palerno up at the Cambria A.C. said of Tiger Tommy, "He's got the name, you know, Dempsey, for Pete's sake, and the punch, but unless he had a personal reason to swing hard, Tommy was no fighter." Tommy's father knew that and got his son out of the prize fighting game quickly. Tommy only had three professional fights. He won two and lost a hard one to a knurly-muscled Black Kid from Baltimore.

=/=/=/=/=/=

In drizzling rain and a grey fog that draped down from the steel girders of the elevated trains on the last Saturday in September, Tom Dempsey sat on his chair beneath one of the umbrellas. The Gypsy kid didn't show up that morning. He would normally never miss work on Saturdays, never late either. The Food Center was closed on Saturdays so he only had to walk from his house near Bridge and Pratt streets. He was back in school and not working weekdays but still expected on Saturdays.

The Philadelphia street lights were still on because of the darkening clouds all morning. Tom had his pipe fired up. Customers were few and far between. His smoke lingered under the umbrella escaping in gasps into the mist of the fog where it disappeared. With the straw hat and the pipe, he looked like a sitting artist, or someone a sitting artist would be painting, a Cezanne, for instance, with the fruits and vegetables posed behind the ordinary but marvelous subject, and the empty wheelbarrow completing the study.

With Tom still on the chair and pipe in hand, an old woman asked for the boy, and two teenage girls seemed to be walking by and looking around the truck and the displays a few too many times. Tom's Saturday morning cash tally was less than breaking even but his inventory, mostly onions, potatoes, and carrots left over from Friday would still be good on Monday; he hoped to move the rest, his perishables, the tomatoes and lettuces and a few of the specials before packing up. He would have been fine with the work and the sitting, but the boy's absence was distracting.

When Sunday came, the next day, the weather had changed to one of those late September sunlit days, warm, hot actually. The brightness of the sun, that brilliant white light, was blinding if you couldn't shield your eyes. About 8:30 A.M. the phone rang in Tom's kitchen and he answered it on the second ringtone.

"Mr. Dempsey, it's me."

44

"Hey, just call me Tom. That'll be fine, Kid, you okay?"

"Yeah, well, no."

"Oh yeah, whatta ya mean?"

There was a pause and somehow Tom expected it.

Then,"You aren't gonna believe this . . .," said the kid.

"Try me," said Tom.

"I'm at Bridge and Pratt and just found out that this is Sunday."

"What?"

"Ya I'm here, you ain't. I'm sorry about yesterday. Gheez, you ain't gonna believe this."

"Whatta ya expect? I don't get it, kid. Whatta ya talking about? Sure it's Sunday!"

"I don't get it either."

"Hey, Chad, hold on, take it slow."

"Okay."

The phone went dead and Tom decided not to speak, but wait for the boy. Before he got too curious about the silence, the boy let Tom know he was crying.

"Chad, whatsa matter? Are you crying, son?"

"Can you come up here quick, Tom?"

"Where?"

"Bridge Street, where we work . . ."

"Sure, I can. It'll take me more'n half an hour. You gonna be okay with that?"

"Ya."

"Should I bring anything? Anything ya need?"

"No, Tom, thanks. Hurry up . . . please."

"Going now!"

Tom parked the truck on the sidewalk where the steps came down from the El Stop. Getting out, he saw the kid walking toward him. Immediately he knew the kid was injured and shaken. He smiled at Tom, but it was not really a smile, and his lower lip was bloody. Touching the kid's shoulder gently with one hand while taking a searching glance at the surroundings for signs of trouble, he whispered, "What happened? Is this why you don't know what day it is Chad?"

"I got it figured out now. I got rolled yesterday on my way to work. It was somewhere near Church Street. I was walking this way, like I always do, but I ended up here, over there under the stairwell. I woke up when somebody yelled at me, afraid I was dead or something, I guess."

"Hey, God, Chad, did he bang you on the head? That'd explain . . ."

45

"Don't know, but yeah it hurts, so I guess so, but they did something else, I'm scared Tom . . .

"What's that, whatta'd they do? It was more than one guy?"

The boy was crying again and holding his arms crossed with his hands cupped to his shoulders.

"You can tell me, Chad."

"Needles."

"Needles, did you say needles?"

"Yeah, two needles were stuck in my arm and my pockets were inside out and my wallet and my key gone. Can you take me to Frankford?"

"Yeah, can you walk? The hospital is a few blocks that way."

"Yeah, I'm walking alright now."

"Let's go."

They walked south slowly toward Frankford Hospital. There were usually cop cars around the hospital but not on Sunday morning. In any case, Tom never talked to cops.

"So they jumped you and stuck you with their damn needles. I'm surprised they would do that, don't know why, bastards."

"Tom, ain't it scary?"

"Yes, like being around snakes, but you seem like you'll be alright now. How much pain are you in?"

"My mouth hurts and my front teeth are loose, I think, but it's my head Tom, that hurts and feels swollen, but I ain't got any lumps."

"Damn druggies . . . cities gone to crap . . . Don't you remember being there all day and all night?"

"No, well, maybe now, it doesn't make sense though. The time is all messed up." The kid looked up at the blazing sunlight, squinting in its brilliance.

"Okay, go easy, the doctors and nurses are good here. They'll help you."

A car with a bad muffler was suddenly cruising beside them, deliberately keeping at their speed. The people in the car were laughing at Chad and Tom as if they knew them. A guy in the backseat, his face out the window said, "You got any more money, asshole?" He and the guy in the front seat passenger side and another guy in the back seat got out of the car slamming the car doors.

The first guy grabbed Tom by the belt buckle and knocked his hat off and, catching it, he put it on and laughed a wide-mouth, howling laugh.

46

Tom said, "These monkeys are your friends from yesterday, aren't they?"

The boy squirmed up against the wall of a building nearby and nodded in agreement.

Tom made fists and the muscles on his neck twitched as did his wrists. The sun was very bright and its light glared an electric whiteness. Above him the structure of the El Train and the walls of buildings and the pavements were baking in the heat. It was midday, noontime in the city and in Tom and Chad's broken world. Tom was knocked on the ground, shocked and face down looking at the shadow of his head clearly defined on the sidewalk inches from his face. One of the three guys from the car was talking his trash talk to Chad. Tom got to his knees and, dodging a kick, jumped to his feet and started walking backwards already balanced on the balls of his feet.

Specifically targeting eyes, as was his instinct, he flung hard punches. Chad watched intently and with disbelief at the whole scene, especially when Tom was hit and with more intensity, then when Tom's powered blows struck. In half a minute Tom could prance before anyone he wanted to hit and he did. All the while Chad, in fear of his life, kept getting blinded by the sun, and every punch and kick that landed on him joined the sunbursts and he felt and saw lightning bolts whenever his skull or face was battered. He swung back furiously and on target nevertheless, until cops were on the scene.

The cops stayed a few steps back from the brawlers at first but soon they began making handcuff arrests. Tom was considered a victim and was not cuffed. Chad was handcuffed first and did not complain as if it made him feel safe, and that it was going to be over.

Unexpectedly, Chad fell to the ground with his first seizure right there on the sidewalk, staring up at the noonday sun directly overhead and merciless with its bone-white illumination.

Tom, moving to help Chad, went to his knees, all his fears over-taking him as he wept for the boy.

The Frankford Hospital said the boy died of an overdose, and Tom, well, Tom got old. He worked the huckster truck for years afterward but never hired another boy, and he left the Bridge and Pratt Streets hotspot for a railroad train station in Elkins Park, a quiet suburb outside of Philadelphia. The boy had a girlfriend who Tom met at the hospital before Chad passed, and then again at the funeral. Her name was Eva and she looked Gypsy and beautiful. She knew all about Tom's fighting three guys to try to save Chad.

47

In the months following, Tom wanted Eva to have all his opera tapes because they only made him sad, but then he thought she might feel the same way so he didn't. He wanted her to hear the beauty of the Italians, as if it was Chad in song about what might have been. Tom sadly realized that all romance and song for Eva was shattered for a time. Eva would come to Tom's huckster truck with her mother once in a while. Tom was glad to have a friendship develop with Eva, especially in his old age. She never forgot him, and maybe once a month, or so, when Tom's age was getting the best of him, she would visit.

When those final heavy doors were heard closing and Tom kept imaging himself as a boy crossing over that fallen log, this time with Eva watching, he would pause each time in the dream and look ahead for Chad. First he would see the produce on display, looking ripe and ready, and then it was the boy. Tom would see the Gypsy Kid listening to him and sitting in the wheelbarrow shaded from the brilliant midday sun beneath the steel girders of the elevated train in Philadelphia.

Erie - Torresdale

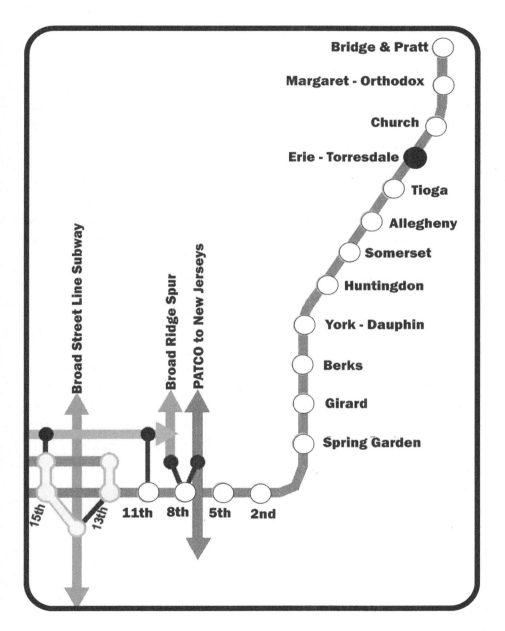

Chapter 4

North Catholic, (Northeast), High School for Boys stood beside the Erie Torresdale stop. Guys who went there never forget it. No matter where they go they bring North with them. Danny always said the same thing. I mean there was pride and tradition. One day we were on the train and it was jammed, and a lot of women happened to be standing in the aisle, and it seemed there was more of them pregnant than usual. Well, the mascot for North Catholic was the Falcon. A guy named Billy Hendrickson, whom Danny had algebra class with yelled out,

"Hey, Danny, there must not be any Falcons on this El Train, cause all these pregnant ladies are standing."

Danny always admired Billy for his football and his manners. Anybody who played football for North was a hero, and North's football was legendary.

In later years he wrote a big story about Billy Hendrickson, an out-of-work, college professor named Tom Montgomery, and another North Catholic alumnus named Doyle. That article was partially published in a series on senseless gang violence in the city. It was a kind of Police Gazette story. I liked the college professor Tom, because he was also a history teacher like me.

Among Day Laborers

Bill Hendrickson says, "I don't care what Doyle says about a lot of shit but he has lived with the Blacks all his life… That makes a difference … like my brother Jimmy says, we don't know nothing about being Black."

He unscrews his thermos cap studying the steam rising from its contents.

Tom Montgomery says, "Doyle claims the perfect Black man is a guy who graduated from high school with good grades, he can hold a job for decades and he has some genuine humility but knows that he is as good as, or better than anybody."

He is sitting in the company truck with Bill Hendrickson. Both men are waiting for Doyle's son to arrive for a day-labor job they got that morning at The Doyle Company.

Bill pours himself a cup of coffee while Tom keeps talking about Doyle,

"Doyle says the religious Fundamentalists are all religion but out of social pressure…. They buy into rules and expectation about how you're supposed to think and act and all that Sunday preacher stuff. Their trouble is, if you ain't one of them, you ain't saved. It's exclusive stuff. Then he says the less or non-fundamentalist types are too protective of their treasures – you know their private lives and accomplishments – and are never truly integrated with the whole Black population, so not much goes back into the rest of the race. Doyle says he always hires the Catholic Blacks because they probably just quietly believe the religion or don't care but somebody in their family history had to make a decision to cross the line in order to become Catholic so Doyle respects the linage, you know the type of Black who became Catholic… Do you know what I mean? Doyle hires people who are partakers, doers of everyday stuff and everyday accomplishments…"

Bill says, "Doyle makes sense. Let's face it. There are Blacks and Whites that ain't worth a pile of horseshit when it comes to being part of the game of life especially in the city." Bill hands Tom his thermos.

While both of them are drinking coffee, Tom says, "Doyle told me no matter how hard some of the women try to change the course of their kids or their family member's kids it almost always comes out the same.

He was on that study outcome… you know, why a great percentage of Black youth fail or drop out or do poorly in the schools."

Bill says, "Don't tell me Doyle served in some sociological study!"

"No, I mean he was criticizing it."

"Okay, what did he…?" Bill stops talking seeing that Tom is looking up ahead of the truck with an expression of focused attention.

"Here comes Doyle's son."

"Yeah, I see him," says Bill.

"He's just a kid," says Tom.

"He's got his work-gloves. That's good."

=/=/=/=/=/=/=

The two men wait for Doyle's son David to climb up on the truck bed. Bill leans out the window and says," Yo, David." Tom nods and gives a slight wave. The young man waves smiling politely and makes his way to the back of the truck climbing up over the tailgate. Bill finishes his coffee quickly and begins driving the truck to the Doyle job site at 6:31 A. M.

The truck had the letters, Doyle's Home Improvements written on both side doors and across the tailgate in bold letters. Doyle trucks were always kept remarkably clean and well maintained. Bill and Tom and Doyle's son, David were on a day job filling the huge hole where an elderly couple decided to give up maintaining their backyard swimming pool. The pool was a large kidney shape with a six-foot-deep end and a three-foot shallow depth. Doyle's estimator calculated that it would take 47 tons of dirt including the broken-up concrete a Doyle crew tore up the day before. The property owner did not want any trucks or tracked construction equipment working on the lawn so the dirt had to be shoveled by hand into the hole. The forty-seven ton load of dirt was delivered to the paved driveway so that every shovel full would be a laborious chore and three men were picked to do the work, Tom, Bill and Doyle's son, David. Bill is the supervisor on all city jobs that Doyle's company contracts. David's father would inspect the work at least once during the day. The men had to fill in the hole and then level the fresh soil.

They each had a long-handled shovel and a wheelbarrow to work with and a rake for the final task. The last part of the job would be the sod crew the next day covering the dirt with grass. Doyle would come the following day and work a roller to flatten the earth himself. It was predetermined that the work of filling the hole would be finished by four o'clock. Doyle would probably arrive in time to make any last minute corrections if necessary.

Doyle was an efficient and fair-minded boss who thought he knew how to work hard, and how to handle workmen. His son was only recently showing up on day jobs. The biggest problem Doyle had was being able to always find enough day laborers to cover the planning of jobs from start-up to completion.

=/=/=/=/=/=

The Doyle truck pulled up the customer's driveway almost sound-lessly except when Tom and Bill open and close their doors. The work-day started with a cool morning breeze and a Carolina Warbler repeatedly crying out its primitive sound at haunting intervals. Three shovels and three wheelbarrows were soon moving at steady paces. Bill and David were immediately moving at a quicker pace than Tom. Tom, slower but not lazily performing his part, appeared less accustomed to the work. They started at 7:04 A. M. and at 9:56 they put their shovels down on the dirt pile and surrounded the drinking water tank strapped on the side of Doyle's truck. David produced an apple, and Tom and Bill had their large thermoses of coffee.

The sun was presently coming in and out of cloud banks. The day was getting hot especially when the sun came out from behind the clouds. The breeze had all but left the scene. David was perspiring more than his co-workers but Tom was visibly tiring and sweaty. Bill had a stiff neck he was favoring. There were no trees around the pool area and none where the truck was parked. The shade trees were many paces from the work. They would only seek the places under the trees when the half-hour lunch break began at 12:30. As they went back to work at 10:14 Tom whispered to Bill, "We're all niggers today."

Bill says, "Tom…" and he checked the volume of his voice and muffling his words he says, "You're working for Doyle… You don't use the "N" word on the job… no way, man!"

"Yeah, I know, forget it."

Bill guided Tom aside, away from David, and spoke in a hissing whisper, "Hey, Tom, when Doyle married Sara Hope, racism became a cancelled ballgame in this company."

David was already on his second wheelbarrow when Tom and Bill started working again. Although the dirt was soft and easy to sink a shovel into, however, tons were tons and the work got harder and harder and the day hotter and hotter. Finally lunch and the space under the nearby shade trees became like something happening on the deck space on a cruise ship. To the dirt-and-dust-covered threesome, lunch on the grass under the trees was a very welcomed relief. Yellow Finches fluttered in and out of the bushes by the owner's house. Tom and Bill both had opened slightly soggy but delicious looking Philadelphia hoagie sandwiches while Sara Doyle drove up and dropped off lunch to her oldest son, David. She handed it to him from her car window. She had a self- imposed rule of never walking on her husband's job sites.

As she pulled away Tom said to Bill, "There she goes."

"Yeah, see what I mean, you talk that racial crap and you're back on the job search."

"Yeah, I know. Look, I've been a history teacher for about fourteen years. I was out of work for twenty-one months before Joe Doyle started hiring me. I need the job," says Tom.

"But you never thought you would be a shovel man… right?"

"Are you kidding, I've got a Masters Degree in American History and I was writing my thesis for my Doctorate."

Bill looks sympathetically and comments, "Yeah, I heard about that when you got hired."

"I guess you should know my paper was on Blacks."

"Blacks?"

"Yeah, I always taught Black history in my classroom. The thesis was on Negro slavery and the impact of malaria in the establishment of the American Hegemony found in post-civil war and particularly in the antebellum period starting with colonial America… Impressed?"

"Impressed, yeah, I'm impressed. Malaria, you gotta explain that connection? I never heard anything about malaria in any American History class I had at North Catholic. You still don't use the "N" word around Doyle."

"No, I didn't mean anything personal. I just don't get real happy digging dirt on hot summer days like I never finished high school. Whatcha say it was gonna be today, 92 degrees?"

David joined them sitting on the grass with his back against the trunk of a huge Ash tree. A Blue Jay made his third trip that morning over the job site.

Bill, still engaged with Tom's conversation says, "The so-called economy has been devastating on people even in the schools which the government said they were going to support no matter what. And here are you with a doctorate digging ditches."

David looking up at Tom with keen interest says, "You have a doctorate, Tom? Whatcha doing working construction jobs… sorry, none of my business… just curious is all."

"That's okay," said Tom. "I was working on my doctorate before

54

I lost my teaching job. Lots of schools have been cutting jobs and mine got chopped."

Bill says, "Tom taught American History before he got laid off. He was into stuff about you Black people and malaria, right, Tom. Tell us. Tell young David here what you were writing about. David is a college student. He only works jobs part time, that correct, David?"

"Yes sir. What was your doctorate on? Or what is it on. I'm sure you plan on finishing it." Robins and Sparrows were landing and alighting on the freshly shoveled dirt.

"I hope so, David. I am doing my sabbatical on these earthly matters as you see today. I do hope to get back to academia when the economy turns around."

"Yes sir. Do you have your thesis in rough draft? Can you discuss it?"

"Yes, there was a threat to white development throughout the South and some northern areas from the prevalence of malaria. White land owners would send their indentured white help over to their land holdings in early America and see if they contracted the disease before they would settle on the land with their families. Malaria killed many of them and held back the progress of the land owners."

Tom took a bite of his sandwich and measured David's level of attention.

"Hey, David," says Bill. "You've got lunch delivered by mama you best get to it."

"My mother likes to check up on me. I think she's worried I'll get hurt working construction. She always rides by or delivers my lunch. She's a good momma."

"Sounds like a good momma," says Tom.

The three sit on the grass even though there were lawn chairs present around them. Doyle employees are not allowed to use customer's property for any purpose.

Bill asks Tom, "What's your paper on malaria all about?"

"It's not finished," says Tom, "but it covers the contribution to the new land by Black Africans who were almost all immune to malaria. If they had not been in America, roads and bridges and railroads and farms and crops of all kinds and livestock would have never flourished. The Black African Slaves built and worked nearly every aspect of Southern development and a considerable amount of Northern economic advancement."

"I had a course on American history last semester," says David.

"I never heard of that account of slavery." A Red-winged Black bird perched on a lawn chair sounded its single chirp alert.

"Where do you go to school, Dave?" asks Tom.

"He goes to Community College," said Bill.

"Yeah, my father wants me to do the first two years in Community College. I've been accepted to Rutgers and Penn. I hope he lets me go to Penn."

"Big money," says Tom.

"That's why I work jobs as much as I can; not that it would make that much difference. Penn is Ivy League and I want that."

Bill says, "Man, I'm surrounded by geniuses but I'm proud of my North Catholic High School education. I took all academic courses and until I busted my knee I played right offensive guard for the Falcons. Nothing like that tough neighborhood ball, happens in the Ivy League, and you didn't need a doctorate, although that was optional, I'm sure. Go Falcons!"

David, smiling says, "Like Sylvester Stallone said, `I don't wanna be just another bum in the neighborhood...' What did the whites do to keep from dying off from malaria?"

Tom says, "Lots of them got sick and died but they did obviously learn one thing to survive. You probably never saw the old movie, *Gone With the Wind* but in that film they showed the white ruling class living in a mansion built up on a hill, with all the shrubbery cleared on the slopes of the hill. The main house was built on a mound. The whites somehow discovered if your home dwelling was laid out like that, people didn't get sick as much, not like those living down on low ground. They didn't know malaria came from a mosquito but they found out something that later would corroborate with the science. Mosquitoes were attracted to standing water to carry out their reproduction. The Whites caught on to avoid living on low lands Anyway they might not have taught you about it in Community College but your Black heritage can boast of being the corner stone of half of this nation's initial infrastructures and its early survival. The South could not have fought the civil war or become a nation within a nation without the strength and endurance of the Blacks." Two crows called from the top of the largest tree in the yard.

David enjoying his mother's lunch and the conversation said, "I never knew about the malaria. That's important information. Thanks for telling us about your thesis."

At 12:32 they stood up and went back to their work. At 12:54 a young Black male with a black cloth tied around his head, gathered at the back and with an earring on one ear showed up at the job site. He drove up in a junky-looking, faded, white Chevy. The car was marked with graffiti. He stood at the foot of the driveway and shouted, "Bill here?"

Bill looked at him curiously and said, "Who are you, pal?"

Looking at David, the young man said with a smirk, "Nutter shovel."

"What?" said Bill.

"I'z sent heres… to work wit y'al."

"You work for Doyle?" says Bill.

"Yeah, whatchas all doing heres?"

"Who sent you here?"

"Doyle, you knows Doyle?"

"Yeah okay, did he give ya a shovel?"

"Yeah… in dah car."

"Get it then, and start shoveling. You ain't got no wheelbarrow, I guess?"

"What?"

"Never mind."

The young man got his shovel. Bill saw it was a Doyle Company shovel, stamped on the handle.

When the young man was on the pool area with them, Tom asked, "What's your name?"

"Duanh."

"What?" said Bill.

"Duanh."

A male cardinal, brilliantly red stood motionless on the fresh dirt. Initially, David didn't look at the young Black man. David made no eye contact at all but kept working as if there had not been any change in the job. Duanh went over to him and began helping him fill the wheelbarrow. A few times their shovels knocked into each other spilling the dirt on the ground. When Duanh's dirt was spilled, he became annoyed and would deliberately bang his shovel into David's a few times. After nearly two hours of silence, except some casual commenting between Tom and Bill, they all took a break. Bill and Tom and David went to the water tank on the side of the truck. Duanh went over under the trees and sat on a lawn chair.

Bill yelled over to Duanh, "Hey, man, you aren't supposed to use the customer's stuff."

"What dah hell you talkin about?" said Duanh.

"The chair," yelled Bill. "You ain't allowed to sit in the chair."

"Screw you."

Bill walked over to Duanh and said, "It ain't me... It's not my rules, man... Doyle doesn't ever let his workers use anything belonging to the customers."

"That's bull, Jack."

"Hey, it's Doyle."

"Screw Doyle."

The young man got up and picking up the shovel he came with he started walking off the job. David was watching him and frowned when Duanh was walking past close to him. Duanh said, "Whatta ya looking at, Jerk-head?"

David looked over at Bill and Tom. He was visibly frightened.

He said, "Tom..." Something triggered in Duanh's mind and he threatened David with the shovel by holding it up high and feigning he was going to throw it at David. David turned away as Duanh threw the shovel at him. David put his hand up for protection but the shovel hit hard below the shoulder blade gashing through his shirt and skin.

David hollered in pain and called out to Duanh, "You dumb bastard."

Duanh stomped over to his Chevy and ripped open the passenger door. He pulled out a dull metal colored 9mm handgun and walked back over to David and shot him twice, once in the buttocks and once in the upper back.

There arose a cacophony of bird noises. David collapsed onto the driveway with a groan and a gasp of breath.

It was the third homicide in Philadelphia that week and the seventh that month. David Doyle was pronounced D.O.A. at Northern Liberties Hospital in North Philadelphia at 3:52 P.M. That was within minutes of the time that Doyle drove to the pool job site to inspect the work and to give his son a ride home.

Sara Doyle was already there walking aimlessly over the pool area's fresh dirt. Duanh was in custody. Bill and Tom were both standing on the grass under the shade trees talking to each other. Tom was weeping bitterly. Bill had blood stains on his hands from trying to stop the bleeding. Before Doyle was going to drive his wife to the hospital, she went over to Tom and Bill. She said to them, "Did he say anything before he died?"

She saw the blood on Bill's hands.

Bill looked at Tom. Tom said, "He called my name, Mrs. Doyle."

She sighed and sat on a lawn chair and began convulsing with tears. Trying to speak but unable, she let her head drop down, her chin against her chest. Finally as if she had to talk about it she raised her head up. Her dark brown eyes rimmed in red, were glistening from her crying.

She said, "What a strange day for him, he told me this morning and again at lunch that he thought he was just beginning to understand that he was a cosmic reality, a part of the whole universe. Can you imagine such thoughts from so young a boy? He was a deep thinker at times..." She turned her gaze away from the men and toward her husband in his truck. "Today was a day for him to be deep. Today came true for... him. Did you see how wonderful he looked when he smiled?" Her head bent down again, her chin against her chest.

Bill said, "Yes, we did, Mrs. Doyle. We got to work with him and we had a conversation, me and Tom and David, right here, just a couple of shovel men. And we know we were with a young man who was truly an important part of the whole universe." He was talking to the top of her head. She never looked up.

Tom said, "A real bad young man came along who had no idea that he was a part of the same universe as David. Neither one of them is extinguished by what happened today. They both go on eternally, one alive forever and one living but dead until he awakens."

It was 4:22 P.M. in Philadelphia. Joe Doyle was still sitting in his company truck with the air conditioner running at maximum, looking over at his wife on the chair on the grass and wondering why there are always two different types of Blacks and why there are two different types of every race and nationality he ever met - good people and bad, bad and good, real bad and real good.

He put his head in his hands and began sobbing, "Why did I hire that guy? Gheez, don't people use their minds to control the bad and think in God's grace." He wanted to go to his wife, to comfort her but he knew she could not be consoled.

Sitting in the truck in tears he remembered a priest at North Catholic telling the class he was in with Bill Hendrickson, "You will be purged in your life and it will bring you to who you are and that you are part of the whole universe living forever."

He wondered if his son ever listened to him when he told him such things. "Where are you now, David?"

=/=/=/=/=/=

Tom saying goodbye to Bill started walking down the driveway, "See ya, Bill." Pigeons were walking ahead of him as if escorting him, their heads bobbing as if in protest much the way women do when in groups chattering some complaint to each other.

"How ya gonna get home?"

"I'm gonna take the El."

"Okay, Tom."

Doyle, seeing Tom coming toward his truck, rolled down his window and said, "Thanks for your help Tom. Do you need a ride? Sara and I will be going to the hospital. They want us there. We could drop you off on the way."

"No thanks, you're welcome. I'm going to take the El to the Police Round House to see that Duanh guy if I can get in."

"What?"

"The murderer... I've been working with the young for years and I just can't do nothing."

"Huh. Tell me what on earth you find out."

"I will. I'm heartbroken... What a great kid you and your wife raised...I'm sorry, Joe."

"Thanks, I'd go with you but I can't seem to move."

"Understood," Tom replied, his voice falling off.

=/=/=/=/=/=

Duanh was in an orange, prison jump suit and shackled at the wrists and ankles. He looked ruffled and the black cloth head wrap and the earring were missing. Two uniformed police stood, one on each side of him. He was seated on a heavy wooden chair. At first Tom was not permitted in the holding area but, recognized by two former students working in the Police Round House, he talked his way into a momentary encounter with the young criminal. He was going to be allowed to get near Duanh, close enough to be heard and seen by the shackled murderer.

Tom knew that he had only a brief comment to make and that, if Duanh was going to listen to anything, it had to be powerful, and hopefully resonate in Duanh's brain long after Tom left. When Duanh recognized Tom, he could see that Tom's clothing still had dirt and dust over it and his hands were still browned by the soil. Tom looked into Duanh's eyes and said, "No one can help you unless you let them."

One of the two police guards looked at Tom's eyes signaling for him to leave.

=/=/=/=/=/=

The next day Tom woke earlier than usual and realized as he made his coffee that he wished all he had to do was to shovel loose dirt and push a wheelbarrow. Instead he cupped the hot coffee in his left hand

and started working on his doctorate paper with his other hand.

Golden finches were investigating the plants outside his kitchen window. He read, "The crucial and providential resistance to malaria by the black race is argued to be the foundation and the single greatest strength of the economy of the Southern States." He sipped his coffee pondering, and then scribbling notes,

"They were the building blocks of the hot end of a new nation... They have to do it again..." He stood up looking out the window. "They have to give up looking for so-called leaders and lead themselves individually out of the traps of their existence. Peace on earth and good-will resisting the horrific malaria of drugs and violence and shattered families and broken education systems. They have to reap what they would have reaped if they hadn't been building a new nation for the undeserving slave owners. No more racial robots – take the higher road every one..."

Thinking of David at lunch, he repeated in a soft voice what David planned for himself, "I don't wanna be just another bum in the neigh-borhood." A mature woodpecker began to drill at a tree high up and at the end of Tom's street. It was like the sound of contractors going to work with their power tools. Tom was weeping again for David.

Duanh was in the State Prison on State road by the river. Nearly everyone imprisoned with him was black. Duanh was angry with every-body including himself. The black race, that was resistant to malaria and could do all kinds of servile labor and multiply even in slavery, was fighting off a contagious disease, self-destruction. The best combatants were the smallest children and high school graduates with good marks and humility even though they knew they were as good as, or better than, anybody.

Doyle was back at his work and hiring guys for day-jobs and Sara would never be the same. Bill was slower in the mornings with his coffee, always glad he played right offensive guard for North Catholic because it made him feel connected to the culture that he wanted to love.

Philadelphia was an arboreal city with a million trees and lots of birds. Duanh hears them in the mornings when he is in the prison yard. They make him think of another world, one that is right there with us if we listen – a world that has its own harmonies and is resistant to any form of self-destruction. He finds that the call of the blue jay makes him want to have a place to go where he won't ever hear a gun go off. He is sorry for himself and wants help.

No one ever wonders how so many different kinds of birds all live together in the same city.

Tioga

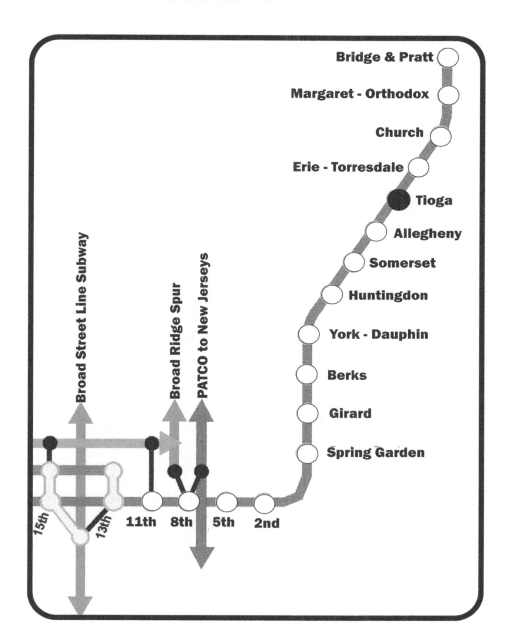

- Bridge & Pratt
- Margaret - Orthodox
- Church
- Erie - Torresdale
- Tioga
- Allegheny
- Somerset
- Huntingdon
- York - Dauphin
- Berks
- Girard
- Spring Garden

Broad Street Line Subway

Broad Ridge Spur

PATCO to New Jerseys

15th 13th 11th 8th 5th 2nd

Chapter 5

For a while, Bridget, Danny's girl, worked in town at the P.S.F.S building until the bank paid her way into Wharton. She started having kids after that but for a year or two Bridget got on the El at Tioga, with pastry for the three of us. It was one of those things that started one day and became a systematic ritual. Danny and I had the coffees from Margaret and Orthodox, and Bridget stopped at Mark Smith's Bakery, "Smitty's" and we ate great sugar on those mornings.

Remember I told you how we Philly guys felt about the boxing especially after Rocky's story. Well, Danny found out about Smitty and he got the story. Bridget set it up, and the rest is boxing history entwined with how Smitty greeted a woman on a train station in Baltimore with a French greeting he learned in a cake decorating class in Chicago. I guess we ought to get to the story before I tell you more about all the boxing stories at the Cambria again.

Pulled Sugar

He was pulling a small sampling of melted sugar into a string of satiny, pearl opaqueness on a lightly greased marble slab using a blow dryer and working under a soiled heat lamp. Stopping, he turned to the sugar still in the copper pot and almost carelessly added some dull green coloring, creating the patina effect he always used every year on the St. Patty's day cakes for the Irish Center. He also did a delightful Christmas Stollen for the German Club and stuffed Paczki, the round spongy yeast cake for the Polish-Americans.

He felt something powdery in his eye and, touching the back of his hand to his cheek, he tried to rub it out by producing tears. He was looking with unseeing eyes at the hint of first light outside the front windows. The friction of his rubber gloves made him lightly punch at the eye.

The candy thermometer he was holding in the same hand hit him on the nose twice. Suddenly, as memories form in the human mind, he saw Blinky Paliamo in his wide lapel brown suit. He was staring at that failed Windsor knot in Blinky's old, eighth-grade, May procession, blue tie. Nothing ever balanced out in Blinky's attire, even his socks never matched, but he knew how to match up boxers, or how to make it look so.

The pulled sugar was forming well under the heat lamp. The jade, almost metallic, elegance of the cake trimming was a perfect base coloring for his bright, Kelly green shamrocks that he would twirl into bigger-than-life, giant clovers. His work was a celebration of green, as if gathered by the wee fairies of Ireland, which is what he always told the Irish Center assistant chefs when they came.

He had a way of putting a story or fabulous history to his work and would spin it off to his customers as he bagged or boxed their purchases.

Still working the pulled sugar, he had another picture of Blinky crossing through his mind. Blinky was telling another fighter, Jimmy Chan that he had to hit the canvass in the eighth in his next bout; Jimmy had a perfect record, thirty-nine wins, four of which were club fight, knockouts, and no losses.

Blinky was telling Chan, "Look, Jimmy you got a great career going, this ain't gonna hurt ya. It'll make you easier to book. This is only your first television show… Okay, Jimmy, okay? You do it, kiddo, and they'll know they can count on you and that'll help ya…"

The first shamrock was too big and he was taking it off when he remembered that Italian guy from Baltimore breaking his nose. He remembered when he quit fighting, he was telling Blinky, "My nose is crooked now, Blink, just like you and the boxing … my father says I gotta quit … "And Blinky saying, "You got forty wins, Smitty, you're one of the best in my stable … Don't quit now, kiddo …"

A simple little cake, topped in pulled sugar, looked sculptured, he knew.

He could see himself being held down at St Christopher's Hospital. They were working on his broken nose. It was the first time he heard the word "cartilage" instead of bone … He felt the pain and tears swelling in his mind just like the night it happened in the sixth at the Lehigh Avenue Boxing Club. He kept thinking about the knock down and how he got up anyway and finished the fight …

The Irish cakes were in rows. "Be few minutes more …" His right hand, the one that put the Italian from Baltimore on his back, wrapped the cheesecloth squeezing the emerald green icing into the last shamrock shape. The bakery door opened.

When the door closed and, as he watched the Irish girl walking away from his bakery in the brilliant, North Philadelphia morning sun, he sat down on his stool by the cash register. He was reminded how his legs were cramped and stiff today ever since three A. M. when he first opened the oven and began his work with the cake pans that had been sitting since the previous afternoon.

Every day was pretty much the same for years now, up until yesterday. In fact, he never had so few things prepared and so much unprepared. But that wasn't the only thing making this day feel so different. He thought, "I'm eighty-two now … I shouldn't be pulling sugar all morning, take the easier way now, you need to go easy."

Then he looked beside the cash register, at the photo that he had put there the day before. The year it was taken was written in ink, hand-writing on the white edge at the bottom. "This don't make sense now … or does it?" He reached for the photo. Looking at it and then walking over to the front window of his shop, he said in a poetic voice, "Put out into the deep,"

A few minutes after ten in the morning, he turned the lock on his bakery's front door. That was often just when customers stopped coming until the busy noon hour. He always closed at 1:00 P.M.

Not today though, he flipped the Open – Closed sign and switched the light switches above the cash register to off. Making quick work of his clean up, he was soon out of his apron and not looking like anybody but an old man walking down the sidewalk on the block where his Closed sign would be a puzzle to his regular lunchtime customers.

Some of the pulled sugar was still on the back of his hand. He had the old photograph in the same hand, "Baltimore, no wonder I remembered getting my nose broken."

Ever since he received it in yesterday's mail, the photo had a way of contrasting incredibly with his present life. In the bright sun of March, it even seemed more dated, more from another lifetime. Staring at his hand, he thought, "like these old hands." Pictured in black and white with hues of gray where all the lighter colors of life would have been, the photo held no present reality for him.

"Maybe," he thought, "coming away from the deep green shamrocks had heightened my senses about the picture… No, it's her … It's because of her. She's doing it. She's the wonder … of it." He was frowning saying, "So pasted to the past." He didn't remember when he began to talk to himself about things out loud. Speaking aloud he asks, "She'll be waiting in Baltimore. Why Baltimore? The airline goes to Baltimore, not Philly, that's all … "

The photo showed her standing beside him when she was nineteen and he was twenty. He was pictured standing slouched, but strong, a feat that only youth can accomplish. He looked tall, relaxed and confident, defiantly confident. He also, at twenty, looked out at the world like the last thing on his mind was time.

She appeared to be on her toes the way young woman do when they are right beside the love of their lives. She was inclined toward him, almost off balance. She was Andrea Pellegrino and he was, Marc Smith, the young prize fighter from North Philadelphia with the tossed blonde hair. It was a very young Marc Smith leaving for the armed services. She certainly looked as if she could never have imagined him as the boyfriend who might never return to her.

As he walked toward the train station and before he placed the photo in his shirt pocket staring at it all the while, he tried to feel as familiar with her image as he could as a conscious preparation for really seeing her. He said, "I can't imagine her looking that way, not now. She's eighty …"

He walked onto the station platform looking for the next downtown train's arrival. The local would take him to 30th street where he would take the Amtrak to Baltimore. Faces of fighters kept coming to his mind, men's faces who would want to hurt him, some more than others. He let himself look at her picture and her face again. A sense of peace came over him. It was a face that no matter how old it had become, he thought, it never was, nor ever would become, an opponent.

He mumbled, and almost speaking aloud about his thoughts, wondered why the days of his boxing had been on his mind especially when he was going to meet her. Then he remarked to himself, "It's because the only thing I ever got out of Baltimore was a broken nose in the sixth at Lehigh..."

He remembered being told by the doctor that they took out most of the cartilage to make his nose straight again. Grimacing, he perked up saying, "I was pretty light on my feet..." The hospital came to mind and he was under a bright light like in the ring. "They just turned my head and held me down ... damn Baltimore again..." He was walking along the station platform.

"Wonder what she looks like? She could be nuts ... No – not her."

=/=/=/=/=/=

She was there, he could see her. She was sitting on a bench with a large blue suitcase and at least three or four other bags. She saw him and stood up turning his way. He had forgotten that he was once so much taller than she and now she looked even smaller. She was very old looking to him and nothing about her looked at all the same.

He was glad he had prepared himself for that eventuality. "He could hear Blinky saying as he always did before a fight and in that feigned intelligent manner, "We must be prepared for all eventualities."

He watched the shrinking of her eyes and how they had changed from first being that of a baffled old woman to being fixed on his as if never to be removed. Amazed at what had just begun seconds ago, he saw how her eyes became jelled and how they wanted to tell him something, something she would have to put in words and quickly. Her lips were twitching as she tried to form words, and her tongue suddenly stiffened unnaturally. She said something, but in French. He was thrown off from his preparedness and disappointed but said nothing. It was as if she called him by the wrong name. Then he remembered what she wrote in one of her letters, that she spoke three languages because she had traveled so much in her life and had lived in Montreal.

He felt as he did when she wrote about coming to Baltimore, "I'm the baker and she is a world traveling, educated woman of much more worldly living than me..." He remembered how the French Canadians greeted each other when he went to The Wenton School of Decorating in Chicago.

"Enchante," he muttered in his North Philadelphian accent. She beamed. He was glad that he had pleased her. In seconds she had gone from incredible old to energetically charged, as if very young, like a masquerading child on Halloween. As she transformed, back and forth fading at once into the old woman and then with a smile, and a nearly perfect row of teeth, she re-emerged as radiant, warmly intelligent and familiar.

"It's her," he thought. In his amazement he noticed how his feet were shuffling around her luggage, and with what ease he stepped forward without stumbling. They came together into an embrace. Everything about him seemed alerted, his eyes and ears, his breathing and suddenly tearing, all of him keyed up. He felt balance and strength, more so than in years.

He held her and put the side of his head against hers as he would in a clinch, more so to regain himself. It was the ring coming back. "I'm getting walloped here," he thought. "It's her ... how'd I get into this?"

The embrace held her back from speaking, kept her where he didn't have to do anything or say anything but he did. He said her name, "Andrea ... "And listening he heard her say, "Lucky." He had forgotten the old nickname. Reeling from the confusion and tone of her voice, his head felt as it did when he would become dazed by the gloves pounding him. He wanted to close his eyes. She was breathing with strained breaths and whispering things he could hardly understand.

Then they were sitting in the train to Philadelphia clasping each other's hand while it pulled slowly out of Baltimore Station. Even with people crowded all around them, they sat silently side by side, both looking pensively out the window not trying to talk over the train's initial sounds. His wife had been dead for over ten years and her husband fell to his death when descending from a cruise ship when she was seventy-two. It was she who first wrote to him. She wrote that she knew he became a baker after his time in the service and that she found him by the name of his bakery.

Looking at his hand, she thought she detected a blemish. The mark was the color of old copper, grayish, green, old looking and a worrisome expression came across her face. She touched the mark gently, rubbing it in a sympathetic concerned manner. The mark flaked off at her touch and noticing it he said, "pulled sugar." He smiled and said, "It's pulled sugar, that's all..." She looked up at him moving upwards to him at the same moment. "It's from the bakery this morning..." he said quietly.

"Oh." She said, smiling through the frown on her old face.

"Did you think I was coming apart?" he laughed. "It's only sugar. I was decorating before I came to meet you."

She smiled broadly and said, "I read all about being a baker, Lucky. There was a part about pulled sugar. I know what you are talking about. That seems a hard thing to do – to pull sugar."

"Yeah, I think I'm too old to keep doing that now."

"Nonsense, I came to help you."

"Pulled sugar is a lot of work and you burn your hands. That burnt a bit," he said pointing to the hand she was still holding.

The train was creeping as he slowly read the last Baltimore sign on the station platform.

For a moment she uttered only sounds and her words slurred like someone dying. He noticed her hand had ceased gripping his and that she was clutching a small silver thermos. Assuming she had fallen asleep, he whispered her name. She did not respond. She was leaning heavily on him. He said her name again, softly but aloud and then repeated it. He looked out the window for a few seconds. Suddenly he turned back to her, knowing that right there and then, beside him, the excitement had been too much for her.

People near him knew it also and they began to react in alarm and curiosity. He held her firmly as he stood, turning her gently onto the length of the seat. Letting her body down carefully, he noticed the train stopping in jerks. People were noisy at first and surrounding him and then a silence came over them with some hushed whispering then more silence. He heard Blinky's pre-fight instructions in his mind, "We must be prepared for all eventualities."

He was standing flat-footed, rocking with the train's jolting motions forcing him to lose his balance, he fell hitting his head on the arm of the seat. Struggling to stand up while a few other passengers were helping him to his feet, he noticed she had dropped the small silver thermos on the floor. He steadied himself against the back of a seat like a fighter on the ropes, dazed and trying to balance himself again.

She had told him in her letters that she was on insulin and blood pressure medicines. Automatically, he reached for the thermos, opening the lid to find it full of orange juice.

He sat her up in the seat and said her name a few times, his voice soft and reassuring. She opened her eyes to his and reached for the orange juice as if in one motion. She downed the juice, obviously familiar with her diabetic weakness.

70

As she slowly recovered, she saw a reflection of the two of them in the train window as episodic parts of their reunion – one of wonderfully connected stories or scenes that were truly only theirs. She looked back at him as he stood leaning on the seat with his knees. She said, "Lucky, thank you."

He saw her for a moment as if all the aging in her face had disappeared and her face was as it looked when he knew her in their youth. Somehow the fainting and weakness of her body also painted her face with the neediness of all humanity and it beautified her countenance.

"I thought you were gone and that I might leave the planet myself. I knew that I would never be pulling sugar again and that the final knockout came out of Baltimore. It was right here," he said holding his head in his hands as if to guard against anymore blows.

"It was in the last round of the eighty-second year of my life, I was losing you for good…"

He had tears in his eyes not at all like the night in the sixth when the guy from Baltimore broke his nose. No, this was a new sense of living and, in an instant, as if sixty-two years could be simply rung out like a bell, he sat down beside her. The fight for reality was over and they were together.

Allegheny

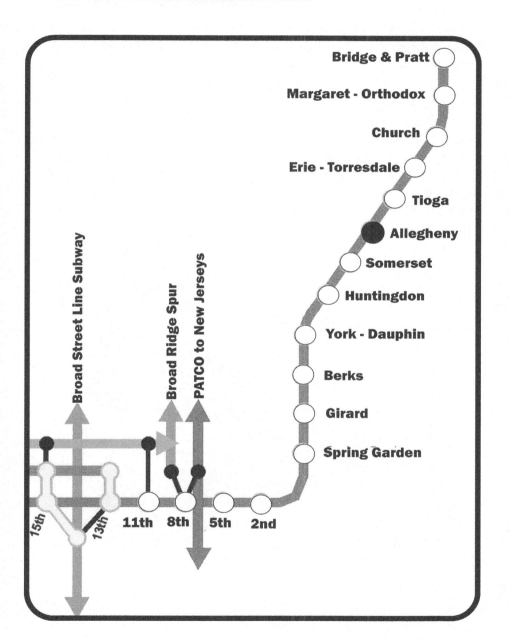

After all the years hanging around Danny and his journalism, you think that you might be able to write like him, if something that really happened stirred you up that way. I wrote a story mostly because Danny Fisher kept after me about writing. He said,

"You could do this job, Joe. You wrote me a couple of great letters when I was in the army."

Well, don't get confused, if this one is poorly written, thinking Danny lost his touch. I am adding this one because it was about the first time I ever saw the El Trains, even though I grew up in the City near Danny. My family first lived a couple neighborhoods away from the El Trains, and we moved near the Fishers when I was about thirteen.

The Lemon Wood Bow

When he thinks back on the days that followed, he sees the dog and him walking slowly casting lengthy shadows over the endless creek as they hobbled along on the stones and ties of the railroad bed. Side by side, they walked sometimes for over a mile. They became healed by the magic of time – just a boy and his dog in the woodlands. Because of the lemon wood bow, he never just bought-into what others were doing without trepidation.

In the wooded areas by the B & O train tracks, hardwood trees and pines and bushes and briars tangled with other shrubs, opening occasionally to verdant grasslands. A small stream alive with frogs and water bugs followed the bed of the railroad for miles in either direction. This is where the dog and he played. It was a fine place to escape from the city streets and to pretend that they lived in a wilderness, and they went there often.

The spring and summer of Joe's tenth year, the dog and Joe often saw the boys with bows and arrows shooting at carefully placed or chosen natural objects. They shot for target practice and bragging rights and, whenever an arrow hit a target, the juvenile archers erupted in whooping calls and proud dances, inspired by the adventurous tales of cowboys and Indians that flooded every boy's imagination at that time.

On more than one occasion, he overheard the other boys talking about the merits of their bows. The single most important aspect of a bow, it seemed, was what wood it was made of. Lemon wood was revered as a material of splendid quality and a bow made of that magical substance was equivalent to the sword of Samaria – only the best would do. The dog had good ears and Joe figured he overheard the boys as did Joe. He assumed that, like him, the dog understood that lemon wood was legendary.

The bows these boys had were real sporting goods store purchases. Joe's folks were poor people originally from the bogs of Northern Ireland so he knew that for him such a purchase was not even a consideration. Still, he began to dream of possessing a bow of his own. It was then that Joe came up with a plan.

For the next ten or twelve months, the dog and he worked hard and long hours at whatever odd jobs a ten-year-old could find. Mostly they delivered circulars for the local grocery store and collected discarded soda bottles for the deposit money. He also began to call sporting goods stores, starting with the first one listed in the telephone directory. Finally, a male voice on the phone answered "Yes" to Joe's lemon wood bow request. A 30-pound test, genuine lemon wood bow was in stock at a price Joe could afford, in a store on Kensington Avenue near Allegheny Avenue – or "K & A," as the intersection was known to Philadelphians.

With his money in an old cigar box beside him and the dog Mickey hovering over, he spread a city street map on the floor. At first the dog wanted to lie down on the map. He scratched out a best spot, which might have been over somewhere they needed to go, and flopped down, but Joe so enjoyed his company he didn't ask Mickey to move. He waited until the dog got up on his own and, when the dog sat beside him, it appeared as if they studied the map together.

Joe emptied the money from the cigar box into his pockets, grabbed some dog biscuits, his favorite crackers, and a pocket-sized fruit jar of grape juice from the kitchen and, with the dog's tail wagging, they started walking.

Before leaving Cottman Avenue, all the dog biscuits were eaten and the crackers and the grape juice consumed. They were well beyond the boundaries of their neighborhood by the time they turned onto Frankford and began to travel deeper into the city. The first elevated train roared by. A thrill snaked up his spine as he realized he was in uncharted territory and his steps slowed while he considered turning back. But the thought of that bow, made of genuine lemon wood, drew him forward, and he continued toward the special store.

They finally reached the place where Frankford turned into Kensington. It was another hub of elevated train activity as the trains flew over their heads with steel wheels screeching and electronic horns howling long and deep. The dog cowered besides the nearest building, whining and quivering with fear. He hugged the wall, his legs seemingly paralyzed, until Joe petted him back to moving. He put arms around him and held his mouth to his ear, crooning his name in a soothing voice. "Mickey, Mickey, we're okay. Be good now, Mickey."

The sporting goods store was wedged between two larger buildings in a very long city block of nondescript structures. It had two expansive front glass windows that displayed various sporting goods, including a few bicycles, a tent, and camping gear. A red kayak, its paddle beckoning one's soul to flee the city, stood chained outside on the sidewalk.

The dilemma of what to do with the dog when he entered the store presented itself abruptly. A street gutter search of about two blocks produced a short length of baling wire, which he attached to the last hole in his belt and twisted around the knob on the door marked use other door please.

As he put his belt around the dog's neck, the cacophony of the elevated subways, trucks, buses, and police sirens was causing the dog great distress. He trembled uncontrollably yet, when he fixed his eyes on Joe, they were filled with complete trust. Joe searched his pockets for any remains of the dog biscuits. Nothing was found.

"I'll be right back, Mickey," Joe promised. "Stay, Mickey, stay. You're okay."

The man behind the counter had the lemon wood bow set aside for Joe. It was only then that he realized he had not thought of arrows. He had just enough money for two arrows and one of those Roman tips, which were the best of all arrow tips. That was according to the boys in the wooded areas along the B & O Railroad tracks, the boy of color claimed they were much better than the standard target tips from the factory. Joe saw an arrow quiver and imagined making his own.

A feeling almost beyond Christmas-present time came over him as the man demonstrated how to string the bow, and his fingers itched to feel it in his hand. He gave his money with pride. He received his purchase. While the man was getting his change, Joe went to the door and tapped the glass for the dog's benefit. Mickey raised his head eagerly and wiggled his hindquarters, his tail almost wagging as he stared at Joe with wet eyes.

Joe returned to the counter and picked up the change and the Roman tip, dropping them deep into his pocket, then tightened his fingers around the lemon wood bow again and carried it jubilantly to the front door. He was now an archer and he held the proof in his hand. He was the proud owner of a brand new 30-pound test lemon wood bow, a bow any Arapahoe or Sioux would be proud to possess, plus two arrows and a Roman tip.

Every block or so he strung and unstrung the bow. On the third block, he strung the bow and shot his first arrow, feeling a light sting where the string hit his wrist when released. The arrow sank into the grass bank on a small row house lawn. It landed with a satisfying thud, and Mickey jerked his head and jumped back. The two and a half hour walk home passed quickly as he practiced shooting, and the dog wisely stayed out of the way.

In the days that followed, the dog took a far second place to the lemon wood bow. Joe had mounted the Roman tip onto one of the arrows, and he spent almost every waking moment thinking of things he could shoot with it. His wrist was reddened daily by the snap of the bow string, until he thought to cut off a piece of an old sock, and wear it on his wrist as a protector. The sock was often still there when he awoke in the morning, though he never intended to sleep with it on.

With all the arrow shooting he was doing, his ability to hit targets was becoming impressive. One day one of the boys in the woodlands challenged him to hit a pack of matches. He placed it on the bank of the stream that ran alongside the railroad tracks, and Joe lifted the lemon wood bow and shot his Roman-tipped arrow. He hit the match pack on the first and second shots. The boy tore a single match from the pack and placed it on the same embankment. He said, "Bury the match in the mud by hitting the red tip." Joe actually did that, and it was then that he knew he could claim his own bragging rights with his own lemon wood bow.

The dog witnessed Joe's shooting with little interest. Often he would find a shallow stretch in the stream to lie down, his stomach on the soft mud bottom, and watch Joe or dragonflies with about the same attention, perhaps giving a little more to the dragonflies. The bow prompted no particular reaction from him, but the arrows were quite another matter. The dog hated the arrows and growled whenever they came anywhere close to him. He snarled at them when he saw them around the house.

Almost a week after he had driven the match head into the mud bank, the dog and Joe invoked the true spirit of the woodlands along the B & O Railroad tracks. In the woods, the leaves at the tops of the trees partially blocked the sun's rays, creating that filtered effect film makers use to dramatize scenes.

Sustained by the knowledge that he had surely gained the respect of the other boys, he stepped into the woods with a true bowman's sense of confidence. He was carrying his own quiver, which he had made out of a discarded leather pocketbook he found in a trash bin. Both arrows fit snugly into the recessed pouch. Mickey and Joe the archer strolled through the woods to the edge of one of their favorite grasslands. The dog roamed ahead of him, sniffing happily along the edge of the briars.

Suddenly a startled rabbit jumped out in front of them, a mere fifteen feet away. As it struggled to find its footing, Joe realized it was caught on the briars. The dog, pointer-like, stood motionless, his eyes glued to the rabbit and his ears pricked. His muscles quivered as he held his pose steadfastly. Before his master's eyes, he was transformed into a noble purebred, a canine prince prepared for any eventuality. The rabbit, on the other hand, was panic-stricken. It kicked frantically and repeatedly, finally tearing itself loose and bounding away, leaving a snatch of fur on the thorns.

The dog glanced Joe's way as if seeking permission to give chase. By then Joe, too, was posed: his legs were locked into an archer's stance, the arrow was pulled far back on the bow string and the bow fully flexed, Joe's eyes were following the path of the leaping rabbit. Interpreting Joe's actions as permission denied the dog first sat, then lay down, resting his head on a front leg and vigilantly watching the progress of the rabbit's escape from the briars.

The rabbit was now hidden by foliage and, had it stayed still, Joe would not have seen it the second time, but it moved. Creeping out from under the greenery, it sneaked stealthily toward what looked like a natural tunnel passageway through the thickets.

Joe's eyes and mind worked rapidly as he saw that the rabbit's escape route would lead to a clear spot that was three feet long with no briars. He aimed the Roman-tipped arrow at the clearing. The rabbit darted through the tunnel and out the other end, and, just as it had buried itself in the muddy earth a week before, Joe's arrow bored into the rabbit's flank.

Joe whooped in triumph, and then he ran to the clearing to admire the kill.

The arrow was still moving, but now only by the quivering power of the impaled rabbit. A small amount of blood oozed upward around the twitching shaft. When Joe saw what he had done, he froze in instant disbelief and gaped at the wounded animal. Mickey ran up to investigate. He placed a paw ever so gently on the rabbit's head, and the creature struggled to right itself. It was then Joe saw that the hole on the side of entry was no larger in diameter than that of the arrow, but the other side was a disaster.

The Roman tip had punched all the way through, splaying open the upper leg in a large, ghastly wound. As Joe stared at the flaps of exploded skin and bloodied fur, he recoiled within himself, horrified at what he had done, and he began to cry. Still holding the lemon wood bow in his hand, heedless of the salty tears that rolled down his cheeks, he knelt beside the rabbit and attempted to remove the arrow. But the wounded creature would have none of that.

It kicked and as if screaming, lunged, making gallant efforts to get away. Joe wanted not to be there, but couldn't bring himself to leave the tormented animal.

Its death took only a few minutes, minutes that stretched out like hours while Joe wept and sobbed out his grief.

When the rabbit finally lay still, the dog nudged the worst part of the rabbit's wounds with its nose. Joe realized the dog didn't connect the rabbit's death with him using the bow. Investigating the magnitude of the wound, Mickey was like a mother dog with a needy puppy. Joe was struck by the native graces of the creatures before him: one showed him the primal raw courage of the woodlands, and the other remained true to his nature and his sense of place.

Joe broke the Roman tip arrow into pieces as he removed it from the rabbit before burying him near the briars, throwing the lemon wood bow into the thickets in a ravine. He wanted to give life back to the rabbit.

In his dreams that night, he remembered just how much.

Somerset

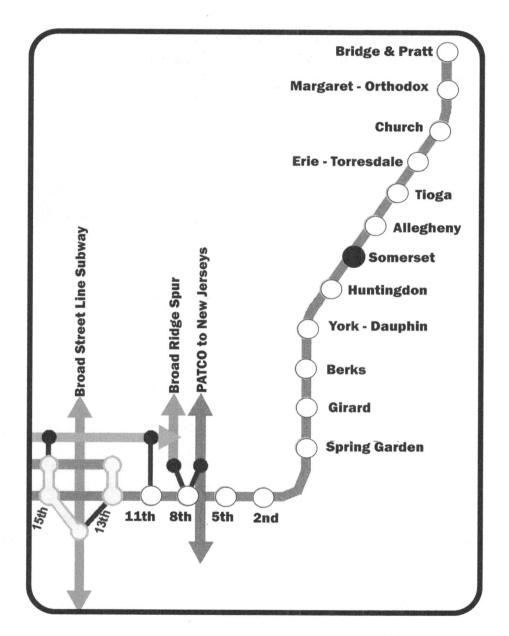

Chapter 7

Danny and I, like all Philadelphians, were always grateful that we lived two hours from the shore and two hours from the mountains, like New Yorkers who go to the Catskills Mountains for family summer vacations and the young adults who, in the winter, go to ski or drink and dance and meet each other — Philadelphians went to the Poconos.

People in Switzerland go to the Alps, The Japanese can be found at the foot of, or in the climbs at Fuji. In Philly you know two things about vacations, the Jersey Shore and the Pocono Mountains. I don't think we ever got off the El at Somerset Station, no reason to, but the name had a spell-casting quality Danny proclaimed,

"Hey, don't it make you think of summertime right away, Somerset, doesn't it?"

"You're right," says I. "It combines the summer and the setting sun in one word."

"That's all you need to know," says Danny. "As the train goes by it, you dream of a vacation. You go to Margate City, New Jersey, and Split Rock in the Poconos, dat's it."

"Oh, yeah."

"Hey, I remember when Bridget and I rented our first cabin around Promised Land Lake. We had about forty dollars more than we needed, and yet we had the best vacation kids and parents could swing."

"Promised Land, sounds inviting, ya think?"

"Hey, you're in the Poconos, what more do you want. The place was near Wallenpaupack, but no crowds."

"Think about the difference between riding this El train and being in the Poconos, man!" I said.

"Let me tell you about a Promised Land vacation, it ain't without what happens on a first family vacation. You know the totally unexpected..."

"Uh, oh."

"Ya, `uh oh' is right on."

The Cabin Fixer

Marty Hagan burned his house down when he was only five years old by setting fire to the contents of the kitchen trashcan in a pile in the middle of the kitchen floor. He lit it with a match to pretend he was an Indian Chief sitting at his council fire. His mother habitually left him alone, exempting herself because she worked seven days a week. She also felt a great need to fit things into her time off, gossiping at the market, for example. That day she almost made it back from her shopping in time to save the house. She always regretted talking more gossip with a neighbor on the way back home that day. She did save Marty though. Marty was always unusually protective of dwelling places after that.

=/=/=/=/=/=

The water in the lake was darkened by the deep black bottom sand and submerged vegetation below its glimmering surface. Dark waters have a surface sheen about them both when they are wind rippled or flattened by breeze-less days. They show a silvery surface, like cellophane or wrinkled tin foil. The sun and clouds, and all other objects, reflect better on dark water. We were walking across a narrow dam near the dark water when we first saw the man who owned the cabin

"Hello," I said and asked, "We drove up from North Philly. Do you know anybody with a cabin to rent here, sir? It'd be great to get out of da city for a week. . . "

The man seemed to be turning slightly to leave. I thought right away that I sounded too much like a city guy. I asked again, "Sir, are any of these places for rent?"

The man was carrying sticks and dead reeds, which he threw down on the shoreline of the lake while he answered, "Well, I never did, but I've been thinking about renting it out this summer. It would be the first time," he said, as he stepped out on the dam to speak to us. "Grandfather Hagan built this place with his brother more than eighty years ago. It has never been rented. This has only been a private family place."

"You're thinking of renting it now?" I asked.

"I might be this summer. I've been thinking about it. I thought about it last year, I remember but this is the first time it would be rented."

"Well, my name is Danny Fisher; it's nice to meet you. This is my wife, Bridget." He gave us a thin, unsure smile.

"What will you want for a long weekend," I asked, looking at the sticks and reeds he had discarded by the dark water. He said, "Wouldn't matter if you rented the weekend or the whole week, cabins here rent one hundred and seventy-five dollars a week in the summer. I want one hundred-twenty for mine. It's little and needs a bit of fixing. I'd fix it myself but everything costs money."

"Well, that's fine," I said, trying to conclude the matter. "May we see your place? We want it for the second weekend of June. It's...."

"Just follow me through the reeds, there's a path. It's grown in, but follow me."

Bridget was ahead of me, behind the man. The reeds stood taller than any of us and were obviously thriving in the mid-spring sun and rains. After the thickest patch the tall grass opened, showing a surprising vista of Black Water Lake and a quaint little cabin. The scene was on the only thumb of land jutting out from the lake's southern shoreline.

The cabin had multiple dormers and a rear screened-in porch with a picnic table inside. The front side had a three-stepped entrance with a little peaked roof over the steps. The path to the front and then off to the rear was flagstone and red brick in complementary colorations. Marty Hagan stood on the front steps, as if blocking our path and said, "Just wait there a second and I'll let you in, just be a minute. I gotta fix the inside door. Be a minute."

We stopped surprised by the delayed approach, since we were all together and on our way in already.

"You couldn't even see this place with all the elephant grass," Bridget whispered.

"Is that elephant grass? Yes, it's hidden. It's nice back here," I said.

Bridget said, "Yes, secluded and a wonderful view of the lake!"

I looked across the width of the lake at the cabins, each doubled perfectly, mirrored actually on the opposite shoreline.

"Yes, for sure. Do you like it?" I asked, meaning to say, do you want it?

"I do...What's he doing in there?" Bridget asked.

"Maybe he's hiding his dirty socks or something."

"No, he's working on the door. I can hear him," she said, whispering again.

"Uhm, you're right," I said, hearing a fumbling sound on the other side of the door.

We walked around the side of the cabin and out to where the thumb-shape of land met the water. It had been a warm spring and the tree limbs were beginning to show their new leaves. With the view before us, I think we both decided on the place without a word between us. We walked around the front. The door was open and I noticed the whole doorknob and lock assembly was lying on the side of the top step.

"Come in," the man said adding, "That door won't lock up again, gotta get that fixed."

"Bad luck?" I said in a questioning tone. I was beginning to realize the man was not good with questions, even little sociable questions, not requiring much of an answer. I decided to get right to the point. "We want to celebrate our twin sons' graduation from high school by taking them here for a long weekend of fun and fishing."

"Fishing." The man said with an acknowledging expression on his face. He drew his lower lip in under his teeth. He looked silly when he said, "I'll work on that dock down there, just needs a few deck boards replaced."

"Thank you, that's good. Do you see us taking the place for the second weekend in June?" I said.

"June, second week, you'll be the first people to rent the cabin, in eighty years. It has never been rented. I'll give you my phone number and address. You send me a check for one hundred and twenty dollars for that week and I'll rent it to you, and meet you here when you come, to give you the key, and all you need to know," he said in one breath.

He looked pensively at the doorknob assembly on the top step. Bridget nodded and I agreed. I shook his hand, and we drove away pleased with our find. Glancing at the man's name on the paper, I read aloud, "Marty Hagan." The name went around in my head over the three-hour drive back home.

=/=/=/=/=/=

The twins managed to graduate from high school, so off we went to our mountain fishing trip to Black Water Lake and Marty Hagan's quaint little cabin.

Of course, like most families, we never do anything without unexpected events. After only an eighth of a mile on the Pennsylvania Turnpike, we pulled over with station wagon, boat, and a homemade boat trailer. One of our four children on the trip, one of the twins, realized he forgot all his fishing gear. So we stopped. We decided the twins would walk back to the house and get the missing gear. We lived right by the turnpike entrance.

While parked there, a state trooper pulled over, and began to question us. Seeing the twins walking down the turnpike roadside, the trooper began to write us up for illegally discharging or picking up passengers. Somehow Bridget talked him out of it. She was persuasive when she wanted to be.

Once again, in less than three hours, we were up in the mountains by late afternoon, following from memory the gravel road to our rented cabin on the shoreline of Black Water Lake. It was late afternoon. So she wouldn't have to cook right away, Bridget had bought two pizza pies and the makings of a salad at a roadside place on the way.

Marty Hagan never mailed us the key. We anticipated meeting him at the cabin as he said when met him in April. Bridget backed that up with a phone call to have him there when we arrived. We found our way to the front lawn and the semblance of a driveway obviously seldom traveled. The tall reeds were already browning. They claimed both sides of the property and more area than I remembered. There was an outhouse, I hadn't noticed before, making me wonder if the place had a bathroom. The door on the outhouse was detached from one of its two hinges and hung on a slight slant in its place.

We were all out of the station wagon stretching and walking around when he drove up in a dented pickup truck with a broken rear window. After a friendly greeting, Marty Hagan reached into the bed of his pickup for a crescent wrench and a box of kitchen sink faucet parts.

We followed him into the cabin. I noticed that he didn't give us a key and that the doorknob assembly was still on the top step, but quite rusted. Marty Hagan pushed the door open, his hand meeting the door where the knob would have been. There was a hole the size of a silver dollar where the knob came out. I started wondering how Bridget was going to feel about no door lock. I'll stuff up the hole, I thought.

Inside the cabin, Marty went to the kitchen sink, the only sink I saw in the cabin. The whole faucet assembly was missing and pots and pans and dishes were piled up on the largest bed.

"This sink's been leaking. I got the parts to fix her up. I'll have it done in a jiffy for you."

Bridget stopped at the door like somebody just discovering they had walked into the wrong house. She raised one hand and gestured toward the bed with pots and pans strewn across it. Marty Hagan had turned his back to us while he examined his box of parts with a prodding grease-stained finger. Bridget, surprising me with her adaptability, started cleaning off the picnic table and setting places for us to have a pizza and salad dinner. I carried in the pizza and salad while Marty Hagan kept busy with his faucet-fixing business.

After we all ate our pizza, we sat at the table for a while. I think the conversation back and forth with the kids and the newness of the surroundings distracted us from Marty Hagan's being there. I may have been the only one to observe him reaching back with his soiled hand for a slice of pizza and nearly dropping the whole box on the floor.

The kids were preparing to play monopoly. The twins were down at the dam, fishing. Bridget was unpacking things and making up beds when Marty Hagan tried his faucet repair for the third time. One of the new leaks was a gusher that sent a rocket fast spray up to the ceiling. It was necessary for him to take the whole thing apart again. He checked his instruction sheet and started putting it all back together.

That fourth time he turned the water on, Bridget noticed, and was carrying the dishes from the bed to the sink in anticipation. The next gusher type leak came out of the pipe connection at the open bottom of the sink bowl. It sprayed Bridget in the mid-section, causing her to drop two pots. The expression on her face was clearly the result of cold well water. She surprised me again by sympathizing with Marty Hagan. It must have been just what he needed because his next attempt was successful.

It was about 9:30 and we had our first running water in the cabin. Bridget watched him washing the dishes and the pots and pans, knowing she would wash them again herself when he left. That's when she realized how much she wanted him to leave. She sent a strong hint when she handed him his truck keys, which he had left on the bed with the dishes. Marty took the keys in a soapy hand, and said, "I'll be back to do a few more things for you in the morning; about eight A.M. OK?"

Bridget grimaced, then with a twisted smile and a few gestures to me she said, "Later, please Mr. Hagan." He suggested, "Nine o'clock," and then he left, pulling out the sock I had stuffed into the doorknob hole.

When the door closed behind Marty, Bridget realized for the first time, we did not have an indoor bathroom, just the outhouse with the door on one hinge. She went out with the kids and inspected it. She came back said, "We can't stay here. The place is primitive." She stood look-ing out the window for a while gradually getting lost in her thoughts while doing the dishes. Then she turned to me and frowned. I was ready to pack up but she didn't persuade me to do so.

Afterwards, we all got ready for bed the way a family does in a cozy cottage the first night. After I turned the lights out, and only dim moonlight came into the cabin, it seemed like no time at all before it was morning, and Marty Hagan was back fixing curtain rods and curtains on the windows, and helping himself to fruit Bridget had in a basket by the sink.

I thought having curtains in a cabin in the woods was unnecessary, but not to Marty. He worked on them for about two hours. One of the rods repeatedly fell off its fastener. He left that curtain hanging on an angle and unsupported on one end. The rest of the windows looked fine.

Bridget cooked breakfast and we all ate great stacks of pancakes with Marty climbing around and hammering. Marty ate at least two pancakes on the job that I saw. I think Bridget actually forgot she was still in her bathrobe and hadn't had time to brush and fix her hair before Marty was once again on the curtain part of his cabin projects.

Bridget did not get much sleep the night before because one of our recent celebrated graduates accomplished what he came for. With the June-born moonlight floating on the night black cellophane surface of our mountain lake, one of the twins cast a selected bass lure into the stilled moonlit waters beside a jutting limestone.

He caught the biggest largemouth bass in the history of The Black Lake. Being a devoted bass fisherman, when he pulled that big mouth out of the lake with his Lucky 13 Popper lure, he displayed his own large-mouth sound, and hollered out a hoot so loud you would have thought he served in General Lee's Rebel Army. That single yell got Bridget and the rest of us out of bed with a start. She didn't seem to get back to sleep for hours. I actually expected Marty to show up when the twins were holding that fish for photos on the front steps at about two in the morning. There was lots of noise made over that big fish.

After breakfast we all left the cabin to further explore the lake and to have some more time together without Marty Hagan around. He had stayed beyond the curtain call, so to speak, to fix the outdoor well pump handle in the front yard. The handle, it seemed, would slip off its pivot pin because the bolt on the end was missing. Down where we were, we could hear Marty occasionally when he made sounds loud enough to be carried out over the lake. You knew he was still up there at the cabin.

Later on we found him gone. There was still the promise of the new morning to explore, as well as our selves living briefly in a cabin by a beautiful dark lake. With nature all around us the hours went by like old wooden boats, their oars stroking as silent as the way the hands move on a country town clock. Sometime after lunch, we got our fishing gear and we all went fishing except Bridget and our youngest son. He was not a fisher-man. They sat on the front yard playing a spirited game of Parcheesi.

That evening Bridget cooked a delicious pasta dinner, and I opened a bottle of South Philadelphia homemade Chianti wine I brought for that meal. While we were out on the back porch enjoying our evening dining atop the thumb of land that pointed out to the lake in an orange panoramic, glowing sunset, Marty appeared at the rear window to fix the sagging curtain. When he tried to hammer a small nail into the mounting fixture, he broke a small pane of glass in the upper corner of the window. He also fell off the chair he was standing on when the glass broke, probably from a fright response to the sound. I remember how we all squirmed around uncomfortably during the remainder of the great pasta meal.

By this time, of course, the look on Bridget's face was telling me she had quite enough of Marty Hagan, but was too polite to toss him out the unlocked front door. The back door was, by the way, all blocked off by summer furniture, and a partially disassembled lawn mower.

=/=/=/=/=/=

Early the next morning, at daylight, before any of the rest of the family was awake, Bridget had to use the outhouse. I was aware of her putting on a pot of coffee on the old stove near the front door under the window with the broken windowpane and the crooked curtain. She took a cup of coffee with her to the outhouse.

When she was back in bed and we were all asleep about 8:00 A.M., I heard the crackling and snapping sounds of a blazing fire. We determined later that the dangling curtain near the broken window had probably blown over the burner the coffee pot was on, or perhaps it became ignited by the pilot light.

Bridget was sure she had turned the coffee pot off. That's what she recalled later when it was all over. We also learned that a volunteer fireman, and a lifelong friend of Marty's, who lived across the lake, had seen a pillar of fire and its reflection on the dark water on the south shoreline. That was the reason the firemen were alerted so quickly.

I was on my back looking up when I woke. I noticed immediately that I couldn't see the ceiling through the smoke since the upper portion of the cabin was already filled with acrid smoke. Hot air was surrounding us quickly. The area around the front door was engulfed in a fiercely flaming fire.

I jumped out of bed, only to be choked, unable to breathe when I stood up. I had to duck low to the floor, where I gasped for air. I woke everybody with a yell, to stay low. The front door was blocked by fire, and I couldn't quite figure out where the back door was. I remembered it was obstructed by Marty's junk.

I got the kids down on the floor. At that very moment Marty Hagan pulled the front door open by the rag I had stuffed in the doorknob hole. That meant that he was standing in the flames at the front door for a second. He had a toolbox in his right hand and quickly darted from view. I tried to cover everybody in blankets and figure out how to get out when the toolbox crashed through the back window. Marty smashed out all the glass and framing and came climbing in. He lifted our sons out one at a time, and I helped Bridget follow them.

I noticed Marty's face was reddened and purple and that the front of his shirt was burnt and smeared with black soot on one shoulder. I climbed out the window last, cutting both of my hands.

We all walked hastily to the front yard looking back at the blaze but ended up at the lake in a primitive sense of safeness by the water. I looked down to see that we were standing on the fishing deck with the three broken boards. There were three new boards and Marty's hammer lying on the ground. None of the kids were hurt and Bridget was only hurt emotionally.

Marty stood with his back to us while he watched the cabin burning. He seemed to be hopping nervously on one foot as he watched. It was like a strange dance, the way a kid might react when excited by something frightening. It was a childish movement by a grown man totally insecure and scared into bobbing like a wounded bird. When I learned later that he burned his house down when he was only five years old, I put the two things together and figured that was probably how he hopped around when he was five, watching his home burn down.

In my memory, I always think of Marty Hagan as The Cabin Fixer. He came that morning to finally fix the front doorknob. Thank God Marty Hagan fixed things by himself, (even though it all costs a lot of money, as he said when we first met him.) The local firemen were able to save that old cabin by pumping torrents of water from the beautiful Black Water Lake right off the thumb of land behind Marty's place.

Marty sent us a newspaper article from The Black Lake area. It was about the Hagan cabin fire. In the article Marty was quoted as having said he burnt his parent's house down when he was only five. He said he was pretending to be an Indian Chief at his council fire on the kitchen floor. The journalist wrote about Marty's heroism and that Marty said, "At last I don't feel as if I screwed up my whole life because of a fire."

Bridget and I often thought of buying that cabin. We never did, even when it went up for sale when Marty died an old man. We simply couldn't do anything that would change the memory for us.

I don't think I could have ever caught up to all the repairs without Marty's help anyway.

Danny was such a totally Philly guy, you know he loved Da Eagles and Da Phillies and Da Flyers and yes, Da Poconos. He was Philadelphia in and out. When he told me about the guy constantly fixing his cabin while Danny and Bridget are trying to vacation, I thought about me and the girl from G Street, When I mentioned her, Danny said, "Didn't Phillip Brown live on her block?

"I said, yeah he lived at the end of the block, in the last house."

With that Danny tells me another story about him and Bridget. It involved a guy we knew, and who we played sandlot ball with. His life was a sorrow, and Danny was always the friend of the down-trodden. The guy later ended up in jail. His name was Phillip. We all called him Brownie. Danny was the last of us guys to see Brownie before he got pulled in... Danny had the last encounter with Brown, but Bridget told that story best and in her own words. Her account shows how Danny really thinks. It went like this:

Extinguished Camp Fires Burn

It had been such a sunlit sacrament of a day, sunlight and breezes in the trees and mirrors of sylvan reflections on the water. Our evening campfire fire could have been hypnotic, just what we needed to bring peace and contemplation to us in the woodland in that last week of May.

Phillip Brown whom we all called Brownie came uninvited to visit us and was sitting at our fire, the open blaze darting lights in his eyes, bright flashes of yellow, orange. And thus his eyes burned and his words, sharp-tongued, flew into the evening that surrounded us. In the end you realize you can't stop others from repeating those complaints that are so injurious to you and to them as well, of course. Philip's scorn and pain like the flames seared our hearing. We were disturbed, our harmony shattered.

Finally Philip Brown gathered his things, emptied his glass over the fire in a hiss, and left in his old noisy car. Danny said as the car rumbled away, "I always thought of brown as a humble color. As he drove up the hillside I said his name, searching for some meaning to offset his agony. "Philip Brown," I said again in a whisper, "I wish good brown-like things for you." I murmured something about the earth and wood, as two burnt logs collapsed into the embers.

When the fire ceased its glow with only specs of red and amber lingering, I noticed the moonlight. Looking up though the pines and the straight, tall poplars, I found the moon, a comfort, soft and silent and seemingly not so far away. Night sounds from the forest soothed my ears and my ears made wonder of each new noise. An unspent piece of wood ignited briefly before it too was reduced to sparks.

Brown was gone. Moonlight was painting the blackness into velvet blueness, almost grey, almost light enough for the search which we humans conjure always about our worlds.

The night itself became hypnotic, the day had departed. Danny touched my hand and it was just the two of us again, Danny and me and the breeze of night that sends us cabin dwellers so willingly off to bed. In the warmth of the blankets, I said to him, "You care about them all, don't you -- Brown and the rest of them, don't you?"

"So do you," He said and we slept soundly then, safe within the moonlight from the window while the sun traveled around the world again.

Huntingdon

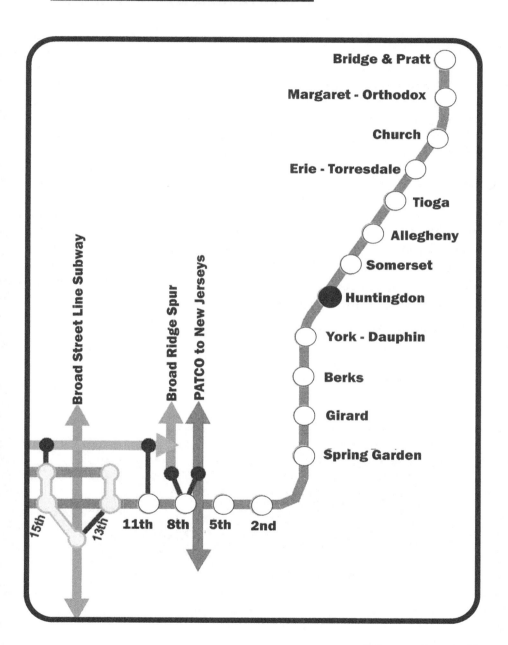

Drexel University attracts many riders to the Market Frankford Elevated. Danny Fisher often had articles published in and about Philadelphia Colleges and Universities. This one was published by, The National Society of Collegiate Scholars, while Danny was doing Masters courses at Penn. The society didn't know that it was a story about a Drexel guy.

Drexel has been a famous Engineering School in Philadelphia for years and years. Danny and I rode with a guy who was awarded the Silver Star for courage in combat in the Vietnam War. The metal was awarded for his calling in an air strike on his own position while he pulled out the wounded. This story about him and his son is particularly important to Danny because the Veteran played Drexel Soccer against Danny when Danny was a right wing at University, and the guy also married one of Danny's oldest friends.

The Wedding Guests

**First published by the University of Pennsylvania
Association of University Scholars, 2010**

As the wedding guests arrived, I found a place at the bar. I bowed my head, staring at my drink. The news that morning about a possible war in Iraq was unsettling everybody. I read the old newspaper article again. It was about us when we were teenagers in Burholme stealing cars and getting in gang trouble. I don't even know how I ended up with it, except I save everything. When I raised my head, I was in the company of my old friends, the ones I grew up with. They were all around the bar and out on the floor. I put the paper back in my pocket.

My friend Greeny's eyes met mine and he unflinchingly said, "We were surrounded by a battalion of N.V.A. I turned and asked the Forward Observer what he was doing. He and I called in artillery. He, the 105's and I got fire in from an Australian Navy ship off the coast."

I hadn't realized he was talking to me. When I did and heard that he was talking about himself in the war in Vietnam, I for some reason, saw us all crouched along a railroad bank in North Philadelphia. We were teenagers waiting to "rumble," as we called it, with another gang. The cops came that night and Greeny and I were running away, I remembered how fast he could run. I saw him with his chin pointed out.

Greeny went on with the story but I was distracted. I was looking at his son's eyes beside him, and the military cut of his hairline and that soldier's posture in the shoulders. His son was busy entering manhood. He had been to Kosovo. He said, "We flew right over the Serbian Army while they were walking out." I wondered if Greeny's son ever ran fast like his Dad did fleeing the Philadelphia cops when we were boys

Then I turned back to Green's face. He looked old. He was older; of course, older than ever, though I still thought he looked strong, even handsome. No wonder he had a girlfriend at his age. We were both in our sixties now.

Then I saw him in my mind with soaking wet gloves squeezed in his hands on the sloping hills of Burholme Park. We were twelve and sledding. Sledding all afternoon, and soaking wet on the soft snow amidst the billows, and walking cat paws of foggy air. We were twelve and it was really all just beginning.

There was the sound of crows, the alarming cry of crows always in the park. They shouted at us over and over, but we were twelve and didn't know they fretted about us.

Greeny's girlfriend came over and stood looking at his son and then at me. I nodded to her and we walked away to the dessert table. I had known her since I was ten. We were in parochial school together. I could still see her in her blue Catholic uniform with her books held against her breasts. She always held her books against her breasts, even later when she was in high school and had breasts.

We picked at the pastries on the wedding buffet, and she obviously looked for her favorite things. Dark chocolates got nudged first, small things with thick soft icing, bitten right in half and one white trimmed swirl of lime green brilliance carried off. After the bites she had discarded the bitten remains defiantly. I smiled at her, recognizing and remembering her playfulness. I thought, "Green's lucky."

When we walked back, Greeny was taking us through the same battle in Vietnam. I was surprised to hear him speak about it in such detail. People think some of these guys don't tell these things because none of us really know what they went through. Maybe they think, no matter what they say to us we won't understand.

"We were deployed perfectly to defend ourselves. My 3rd Platoon was in reserve so we had our rear covered. They couldn't just get around us."

I started thinking about him having gloves in the cold snow when we were twelve in 1955. I never had gloves. My hands were always reddened and biting cold all the time. Maybe he had better parents so he had gloves, I thought. Maybe that's why he went to Vietnam, because he was the kind of guy who would have gloves and artillery fire and the things he needed wherever he was. Maybe I didn't go to Vietnam because I wouldn't have had even bullets or artillery or naval ship fire.

It is strange how your mind works. I saw the dessert table being blown up by 105 rounds. His girlfriend was looking and I knew she would have laughed if she saw what I was thinking, all those cakes and pastries flying around.

His son said, "We met with all the children when we marched into Yugoslavia. They greeted us as heroes. We even cried with them. No one could beat us. We were linked to each other, we knew it."

I remembered how we all walked home from those sledding days in Burholme Park. For a moment while Green talked to his son about war and soldiering, I drifted to one of those walks.

Something I didn't want to have happen was happening. I was going back into our past, that untouchable youth before the great shocks. I wanted to deny or eradicate us as serving Spartans or pawns of the empowered classes and corporate politicians. Something seemed always to cancel those thoughts out, but this thinking had energy.

The two veterans kept me in their conversation, acknowledging my time in the Infantry, and my unfortunate involvement with nuclear weapons. I think they had to tell some stories to each other and I facilitated their exchange.

It was important. You could see that in their eyes as plain as sunshine. I was glad to help them but I was walking far away at the same time, walking down the tree-lined path to our streets, those streets in the neighborhood. Sloane was there and Big D and Mickey, Brownie, Ed Drake and me, Danny Fisher. We were smoking the same cigarette, passing it around, a Camel.

Donna and the two Mary's were sitting on our sleds, letting us pull them along home. Nails and the Forward Look was half a block ahead with Johnny Mac whom we called Jimmy Dean. They were all there in my daydream, and they were all around me at the wedding except Big "D" and Sloane. They had been killed.

Greeny said, "We slept the next day for hours, right in our position. When we woke up and had to write the report, the Forward Observer said, 'God, did we do all that?'"

I said, "Yeah, we had to."

"Anyway," he said looking at me, and then his son, "we couldn't believe all we had done."

His son was facing me and sharing his impressions of his father in a combat zone some thirty-five years back in our time.

Greeny turned and walked off a few steps. I heard him call over to the bar, "Mary, c'mon." She looked toward him, her pocketbook held against her breasts, and a drink in the other hand, smiling. The same smile, the smile all the way back to the sledding when the crows tried to chase us away from the foggy air.

That was when it all began, when we were all twelve years old in Burholme. Before anybody could put us into ranks, we knew how to just hang out, loving each other. You could have saved the world with the likes of us and maybe we have.

Greeny's son moved his wheelchair over to the bar and ordered a glass of water to help him with his pills. Greeny fingered the back of the chair gently kicking at the wheel with his oversized shoe which he wore since recovering from a Viet-Cong booby trap wire detonation somewhere north of the Mekong Delta.

As I watched, I wondered if either of them, or anyone, would ever believe the health injuries from those senseless discreet nuclear tests. I remembered the tests on Nevada's lower basin far from Vietnam, or Serbia, or any other future nightmare.

The band playing for the wedding began their first set with a song from the fifties, when we were all kids, in that brief time between all the damn wars.

"Imagine," I thought, "if we had instead, stayed at peace over the last fifty years, we might be getting used to it by now. Our biggest memories," I realized, "would be stuff like running from the cops, falling in love with someone like Greeny's girlfriend, having kids like Greeny's son, and sledding all day on the slopes of Burholme Park."

When I met up with Danny again, I gave him back his army story.

"Do you wanna read another army tale?" Danny asked.

"Yeah," I said.

"It is a story I wrote for a literature class when I was fresh out of the Service. I think only you would read it the way I hoped it would be read. I got a good mark for it, but other than the English Professor at the University, up to that point I never told anybody about this story and a lot of other things in Nevada. It was really still Top Secret back then. I guess that's when I was first brewing up my defiance.

When I read it, I spoke in my Philly accent and said, "Dis oughta be part of a novel, better, a movie man!"

Neither one ever happened yet, but it was a compliment that I'm still glad I gave him.

In Military Handcuffs

The armored personnel carriers moved up in front of them, the noise of their diesel engines initially, somehow unnoticeable. Joe sensed something like an invisible being in the trench with him. It was as if he were two people now, the person before the radiation and the invisible person or spirit that was either still Joe or some angel he would need.

He dismissed it in the increasing rumbling of the armored personal carriers squealing and opening their steel doors. The irradiated soldiers ran onto the hydraulically controlled boarding ramps, which opened without any human hand touching them. When loaded, each vehicle closed its ramp swallowing the men in a macabre scene beneath the mushroom cloud. The dusty tracked vehicles spread out along the way and dropped their captured human cargo out on the test range.

The head of the mushroom cloud, elevated by a great black mass, black like an empty mine shaft opened to the darkness of the universe, began to fall down range, tumbling over towards Master's platoon now dismounted from their armored machines.

The charging soldiers on foot again were now much nearer to ground zero. They ran, some leaping over smoldering fresh craters and rivulets of flowing, black-crusted, molten, red-fired earth. Soon they met another life form that had been routed before them. Western banded gecko lizards seemed to be everywhere and in great fright.

From above their movements would have looked somewhat alike. Each ran in spurts and after each sprint, the men fell into feeble firing positions, while their counterparts advanced: soldiers and lizards. Finally the forward charge ended for the soldiers. The lizards kept going. In the distance, the horizon seemed to know the innocent would be coming.

Three miles back the perpetrators sat. The Secretary of State repeatedly stroked his hair, his habitual personal tic, but no one near him could tell what he was thinking. As always he looked innocent and thoughtful, his eyes always promising something.

Still out on the nuclear range, Joe, noticing a cut across the back of his right hand, spontaneously calculated how much it would bleed without being attended to. He was up and walking, hot and sweating through the irradiated dust covering his face, neck and hands and clothing,

He hiked up his Browning automatic rifle and cradled it in his right hand. He then grabbed the back of his bleeding hand with his left palm instinctively pressing the cut. After a few seconds, he lifted his palm and looked. Suddenly he remembered his father's stories of the Second World War and his father's scarred hands and imagined the amount of blood his father must have dealt with when he was shot by the Japanese during the battle for Okinawa. He felt the link; father to son, soldiers linked by blood and bleeding. The bleeding stopped. The dust had formed a seal but he still wondered how and when he had cut his hand.

For the second time that day he thought of the Japanese in the atomic bombings at the end of his father's war. He imagined people helpless in the scene he had watched during Tuesday's blast. The names of the two Japanese cities were whispered over his lips. "What have we done? What are we doing now? He thought. "Holy gheez, nobody's gonna believe this!"

Just then Sergeant Masters waved his troops to a halt and when they all stood still and as some of them dropped to the ground, he moved curiously on ahead. He nearly disappeared over the crest of a slightly elevated desert landscape to their front.

Masters started blowing a whistle. As he walked back to stand on the higher ground, his radio at his mouth, suddenly some civilian men came to where he was. They were obviously Indian tribesmen with long hair braided over their shoulders. Three jeeps and an army ambulance made their way through the dumbfounded troops gaping at the scene. Soldiers, way off in the distance could see the commotion but could have no idea what was transpiring.

One of the jeeps had two men in silver protective clothing. They immediately began to take radiation readings off the Indians. The injured Indian man got their full attention first. In the meanwhile the ambulance with its big red crosses got the attention of soldier's eyes all over the desert. Four M.P.'s with .45 caliber side arms produced handcuffs. The Indians were shackled, even the wounded man. All the time, Masters was walking from Indian to Indian. He shouted to one of the Military Police, "Hey, go easy there, Specialist. These men are here by accident or they were uninformed about the test today. It's their land. You don't need cuffs. No cuffs!"

Masters' orders were being ignored. He yelled again, "Forget the cuffs, man. You can see their harmless, you dumb bastards... I'm telling you this is their damn desert you're on."

An officer in the military police, field grade, pulled up in a fourth jeep with his driver. He stood directly in front of Masters and said, "You can go back to your platoon, sergeant. We have this contained now."

Masters, his eyes bulging stood his ground. The unmistakable Cherokee profile of his nose glistening in the brilliant sunlight stood out like the edge of a lance.

"You're done here, sergeant," said the officer, a major in an M.P. company. Obviously reading Masters' name off his uniform, he added, "Sergeant Masters."

Masters kept quiet, staring at the major's M.P. armband.

"Move on, sergeant!"

The Indians were crammed into the ambulance under armed guard. The jeeps drove in front and behind the ambulance. The officer, in his jeep, took up the rear of the small caravan.

Masters quickly getting control of his platoon, said, "Show's over! Don't bunch up! One A Bomb will getcha y'all," he said with a sarcastic African American tone. "Saddle up! Move out!"

Joe was walking head down in his overheated daze. With the mechanical, rattlesnake sound of the helicopter blades waffling in the desert air, he again sensed something.

He looked up and again he saw the two men in silver, full-body, protective clothing. Just behind the two men, the M. P. Major was standing with his arms folded. Suddenly Joe remembered seeing him in the civilian cafeteria when they first arrived at the nuclear testing grounds. The Major was standing beside a civilian-looking man in fatigues who was the blond-haired man with the tattoo who had given them the atomic bomb speech before they watched the first bomb being detonated. The Major had his arm on the other man's shoulder as if to praise him.

Much closer to Joe, the two men standing in protective clothing had formed a foreboding gateway for the soldiers to file through. They held Geiger counters against each man as he passed, probing legs and upper bodies and calling off to each other the Roentgens count. Joe passed through the men in silver, their suites reflecting brightly in the desert sunlight. "This is science fiction. They're like Saturday matinee aliens," he thought.

Joe continued watching the M. P. Major and the other man, the scientist with the tattoo. The Major and the scientist were side by side in conversation, walking towards their vehicles. Another soldier, Daniels the mixed-race boy who was, like Joe, from North Philadelphia was looking around the desert scene for Joe's whereabouts. His brown skin glistening like wet wood in the bright sun. He noticed that they were segregating those in need of decontamination by directing them off to the right side.

He saw that they were letting the greater number of men gather on the left. Sergeants were assigning details to sweep off the armored personnel carriers with brooms appearing out of nowhere. The diesel engines sounded very loud again. A Mexican American soldier, Garces from California, was already up on one of the armored personnel carriers with one of the brooms.

Joe standing on the ground picked up a broom and started sweeping the olive drab steel but stopped when Daniels came over to take the broom from him. Daniels also waved at Garces to come down. In reply to Daniels' suggestion, Garces, always joking, flicked some of the dust at his friends. "Get off of there with that stupid broom, man. Garces, the whole thing is radioactive, you dumb shit. Didn't you see those Indians? They were already messed up. Do you want more of that crap on you?" At that, Joe jumped back afraid of the dust.

Joe and Daniels walked a good distance away from the vehicles.

Sergeant Masters, watching it all, stood uncharacteristically still in the distance. He thought, "It truly is 1962 and the Fourth Infantry is now prepared for nuclear war at the expense of many and this desert land as well. Human beings are the dumbest monkeys ever created. God help us…"

York - Dauphin

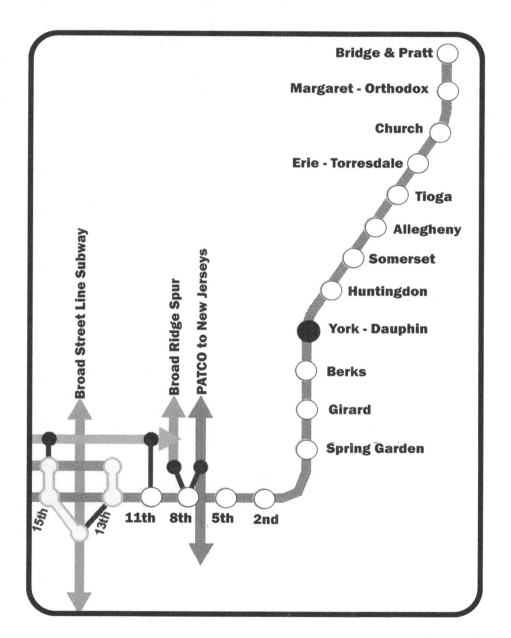

Danny and I got off a stalled train thinking of smoking until the train moved again. We were on a bench seat near the end of the station when the train pulled away unexpectedly. We were near where the first car of the next train would stop, when a gaggle of Boy Scouts marched across the platform. They were wearing their full uniforms and carrying various gear and backpacks. It was obvious they were all aiming to get on the lead car.

Danny was smoking and drawing in a deep drag with which he blew smoke into the morning air and said, "You know I was in the Boy Scouts for the shortest time ever recorded in that Troop. I was in and out faster than you could say the Boy Scout Oath.

Danny waited as the Boy Scouts went off to the very front of the train station, where they could all try for the front window of the lead car. As the next train pulled in, he said, "This isn't your traditional Boy's Life, Boy Scout story, man."

"Yeah?" I queried as we made our way to a good seat.

Danny took out a spiral binder of papers from his briefcase and held them on his lap while he began his tale of The Boys Scouts of North Philadelphia...I looked straight ahead, as I always do, when Danny was spinning yarns on the El Train rides.

"My neighbor helped me go to a Boy Scout camping trip one time. I went with only an old army blanket and safety pins for a sleeping bag. The only part of the Boy Scout uniform she could afford to get me, all the way down at 8th and Market, was the red neck bandanna with BSA written on it and its clasp. I felt wonderful about both of her contributions. And her husband left the bar stool he always sat on at the Five Points Tavern and strode down the avenue with me where he paid the 50 cent fee for me to become a Boy Scout. That was the only walk we ever took together.

"That was non-parental involvement at a maximum in those times and, in my immediate culture. I was impressed by their interest in me and I realize sixty years later they were life-changing experiences. They were richly genuine and they came in small packages back then. The test of worth is how long they are remembered.

"To make the story not about me personally, I changed the parts that would identify me or the woman. Here is how it was printed in the Editor's version."

Danny flipped through the binder and handed it to me open to a page that had the title:

The Red Scarf

With only an old army blanket pinned together as a sleeping bag, the boy was the most impoverished camper among the Boy Scouts camp.

Josephine, the red-haired Irish woman, lived in the small flat downstairs. The boy was the only child of Josephine's neglectful, upstairs neighbors. Josey helped the boy go on the Boy Scout camping trip. It was a sweet time between them. The only part of the Boy Scout uniform Josey could afford was the red BSA scarf and its official Boy Scout Clasp. The week before, Josey's man friend Felix, prompted by Josephine, left the bar stool he often sat on at the Five Points Tavern, and strode down the avenue with the boy to the Boy Scout's meeting place. There, he delivered a paper signed by one of the boy's parents. Felix paid the fee for the boy to become a Boy Scout.

At the camp, it rained all night and the homemade sleeping bag got so wet the boy had to sit up in the dark tent to try to keep dry. In the morning, the Scout Master had a smoky fire burning nearby that the young boy went to for warmth. The Scout Master, shielding his eyes from the smoke, and speaking in a tetchy voice, sent the boy to a supply cabin on a far off hill to fetch a Left Handed Smoke Switcher. The boy was sent from the cabin to a few other places by adults until, after over an hour, it became obvious that he was the brunt of pranks.

The boy, still shirking from all the unwanted interest in him, told a frowning Josephine about the Left Handed Smoke Switcher. He saw Josey tightly folding the red scarf she had washed, and cuffing it, she slipped it into her pocket.

"Are you gonna keep the scarf, Miss Josey?"

Josey angered, squeezed the scarf in her pocket as she said, "I think you going to Boy Scouts shows how we are all born totally innocent, but not dumb, one overnighter is enough for any Scout."

Years later, whenever the boy confronted scoundrels, something alerted him, and immediately he was prepared, like a red flag went up. Often his reaction was accompanied by a vivid memory. He would remember the Irish woman's caring smile as she stowed the red scarf in her pocket never to be worn again by the boy.

Derailed train at York & Dauphin 12-27-61

Berks

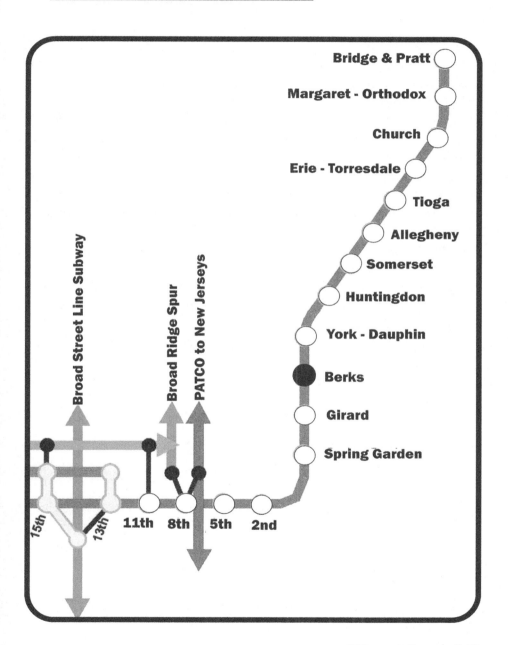

All those years that I rode the Frankford Elevated Trains and talked with Danny Fisher, I couldn't possibly remember one-tenth of the stories and news items we discussed.

We talked about the neighborhood and current world events for sure, but it was Danny Fisher's storytelling that haunts me all these years. Maybe because the El Train rides otherwise got so solitary, my memories of the good stories and the shockers keep coming back to me.

Now every time I pass through Berks Station on the speeding El Train, the story of David and Luke Gantry is bulleting at me as if it was written on the El Stop walls.

My interest, when it came to this story was that, when Danny was a draftee and a Private in the army, he was a jeep driver for a colored officer, a Chicago kid who was an ROTC 2nd Lieutenant named Luke Gantry

Danny said the story of Luke could change history, so that's why he wrote it he said, but added that history didn't change. I wanted to know the history.

Sweeping Enrichment

David Gantry was Luke Gantry's father. David was employed by the Manhattan District plants. He worked, at different times, throughout the early forties, at five of the plants in the Tennessee Valley, and he was retired from the seventy-square-mile plutonium-making complex, whose location and function were classified information. His first employment was in their home town of Chicago, where the untoward incident of the first chain-reacting pile was marked in nuclear science's modern history.

Mr. Gantry was a janitor and, because he had security clearances at the highest level obtainable for a manual laborer, he was asked to follow the scientific developments from plant to plant. Different emphasis demanded geographical moves into newly designed labs and experimental working processes in places chosen for their significant match to diverse and, of course, secretive science. David Gantry went along. All these authorizations were done as top secret projects and the idea of finding manual labor at every location was a tedium the nuclear mission organizers tried to simplify.

Finding janitors was hardly a consideration among those devotees of isotope separation. So many times over it was David Gantry out there sweeping and cleaning in the midst of unimaginable experimentations. Mr. Gantry wondered what all the talk about enrichment was. However, his ability to perceive and be motivated by moral or ethical principles about the goings on beyond the dust and debris he controlled daily seemed to be filled with suspicion, and far from the meaning of the word "enrichment."

In the early years, however, he was impressed and hopeful about his employers and his superiors as they were titled. His task was to be in unspoken service to the elite around him who had credentials connected to the largest, most renowned corporations and universities in America and, walking among them, all were men in starched and pressed military uniforms with Field Grade rank.

David heard conversations and threw papers away that held references to such things as, "equilibrium time, yield, separation factor, and the centrifuge or thermal diffusion." Equations were always left scribbled on chalk dusty blackboards he erased and cleaned when told to do so. He eyed countless equations, mostly on discarded scraps of paper, or pages from notebooks all left under his management.

He would occasionally read something that would become slogan-like and lodged in his head for a day or two or until another phase would replace it. They were always of a scientific nature, such as, "The diffusate will be enriched in U235 F6 by a factor..." His chanting to himself these vagaries from the intellects he served helped him feel smart and kept away the impinging humiliation and occupational boredom.

He also thought all the security taboos stimulated his sense of defiance toward it all. The utterances jumped into his mind and, as he repeated them, he felt like he did as a boy jumping on the merry-go-round without paying for the ride at the fairgrounds back home in Illinois. That was when the white majority segregated him and he first realized that he was a negro boy.

He was preparing his things, a stepladder and rags and solvents to clean the glass windows and the shelves and floors in an in-plant office and he was reading discarded notes in the trash. There was a list under the barely legible heading, molecular weights. The page was filled with fractions and algebraic-like formulas in which the letters "r" and "i" were repeated everywhere. He had thrown all of it in a trash container to be burnt when he noticed heavily inked black letters that read, "Major General L. R. Groves."

Whenever Mr. Gantry got to go home to Chicago, he was never able to talk about the secrecy of his work with anyone, including his wife Elizabeth and his children. He did try to tell his older brother Jerome but he never found the words safe enough to use to explain what he wanted to share. He rehearsed sentences he thought vague enough to get something about it across to his older brother. There was never really anything said more revealing than, "I work for the government."

His older brother was left nearly deaf from the shelling in France during the First World War and therefore any enunciations of words that were muffled or said with hesitations were obscure to Jerome's ears. David Gantry's job was always a lonely occupation, but it paid the bills and educated his children.

His youngest son, Luke even went to college. Luke became the first college graduate in the Gantry family dating back to pre-civil war history. It was not until Christmas of 1944 that David Gantry made a wholehearted effort to tell his older brother Jerome just what David was experiencing.

"Sounds like those poison chemicals again, probably worsen than the ones back in my war, "Jerome said, frowning and straining to hear his younger brother.

"You got it, they are all from the biggest corporations you can think of, and universities, big outfits, Westinghouse, DuPont, Princeton, The Bell Lab scientist, and all around the place you see military men in starched uniforms. They got stars and eagles on their uniforms, all the brass, you know, the big officers rank. They are into the secret weapons and, Lord knows, what that means, brother."

David's throat tightening and his voice was ready to tremble, decided he was not going to say any more about his secrets, but concluded timidly with, "They seem crazy and something about it is evil, I know that. They always talk in whispers about a bomb, by Jesus, it must be da biggest, awful-lest bomb ever made."

His brother uttered a long breathless, "Humnn." and then he spoke about the war in 1917 which he almost never talked about in detail, "You wouldn't ever believe what we done to each other in those God awful trenches. When they brought up the brand new French Artillery, we gave them Jerries hell on earth, and they threw their poison gas at us. I had to watch my mules dying and boys, just boys, dead by the wagon load day and night." He touched his ears with his hands and continued, "They love their weapons and there ain't nobody gonna stop 'em, no stopping that kind. They make each other terrified, and then they share the big scare with each other. Most of 'em are Germans and the smartest scientists, Jews, some of them were trapped, for the love of God, they ain't ever done killing each other and being kilt. They are gonna kill the Japs and we're all gonna kill them, and cheez...."

"They're crazy, Jerome, and like you say, ain't nobody gonna stop 'em or the ones doing it in Europe and the people in them other foreign countries."

"You're cleaning up after scientists makings a mess for the devil."

=/=/=/=/=/=

Eight months after Christmas 1944, Hiroshima and Nagasaki were bombed into annihilation, and Cory was retired by the government. Seventeen years after that, David Gantry's youngest son, Luke was a 2nd lieutenant in the army infantry. He was an ROTC and Officers Candidate School graduate and one of the few black platoon leaders in the whole 12th Battle Group, which only had two black lieutenants – Second Lieutenant Luke J. Gantry, arriving with the small gold bars on his shoulders had a jeep driver assigned to him named Pvt. Daniel Fisher.

Luke soon joined a detachment ordered to ship out to the Atomic Proving Grounds in Nevada. He was to lead his newly formed 3rd Platoon, all of which had to clear Top Security investigations. His father was becoming an old man when Luke was secretly exposed to two atomic bombs as part of a live-fire tactical exercise to prepare combat soldiers for nuclear warfare.

Twenty six cancers were listed on the V.A. forms and government legal documents regarding claims for troops in ionization-radiation experimentation, which also referred to occupation forces entering Nagasaki and Hiroshima at the end of World War II. The language stated troops as far off as 75 miles from Nagasaki or, from Hiroshima, 150 miles would be eligible for V.A. benefits. Thousands of test participants were dead or sickened by the time Luke discovered his maladies. Luke's time for cancer suffering happened when he was the same age as his father was when he was an atomic bomb secret clean-up man for the mad scientist, as he called them.

Before he died, David told his son Luke, "If I'd knew they was gonna get you with their damn acts of hell weapons, I'd of burnt the places down and saved you and the world, son. There ain't nobody ever stops em, Luke."

Luke slowly died of a rare form of gonad cancer and David and Elizabeth Gantry buried their youngest son a short time before David himself succumbed to death. David's older brother, Jerome Gantry lived on to be ninety-eight. After the burials, Jerome sent a letter to a big Chicago newspaper. He was stone deaf, and almost illiterate at the time. He asked his Pastor to help him compose the letter. The letter was a full page but only 45 words were directly from Jerome's mouth. The whole letter was formatted and typed by Pastor Warren M. Jackson, Minister, Hosanna Baptist Church.

Dear Editors,

My nephew, ex-captain Luke Jerome Gantry, died recently of cancer from his exposure to atomic bombs at the nuclear test sites in Nevada. His father, my brother David Gantry was a janitor in what became known as the Manhattan Project. It turns out that cleaning up after mad scientist became more dangerous for him because the real dirt, (atomic bombs), they created was never trashed.

Having been to the trenches in the First World War, I don't have a lot of faith in our prospects to end wars and to destroy our weapons. My brother felt betrayed, He could never reconcile that, seventeen years after Nagasaki and Hiroshima, his son was deliberately ordered into a blast area of two atomic bombs in the preparation of future nuclear war.

My young pastor is helping me compose this letter. When I should have been in school learning reading and writing, I was a young soldier in France, driving mules hitched to ammunition wagons, which became filled with dead bodies from the trenches. At the time, the water- cooled machine gun was the weapon to end all wars.

It has struck me recently that the only weapon to end all wars is for all of us to beg God to concede that gift to humankind. We need to be granted the miracle of the sweeping enrichment of all human beings, and only God can do that for us.

Jerome Gantry

=/=/=/=/=/=

Danny Fisher told me that the letter Jerome's pastor wrote was printed on the fourth page of the Tribune's editorial section under the heading, "Sweeping Enrichment." He showed me a copy of the letter when he told me the story.

I want to remember Danny's stories, and they still come to mind almost as vividly as when he would tell them. Today I got off at Berks station for a few minutes, and sat on a bench and wrote this one down for posterity, and for Danny who was probably the best news journalist in Philadelphia

As for me, I teach my history classes with a whole different understanding of the Manhattan Project.

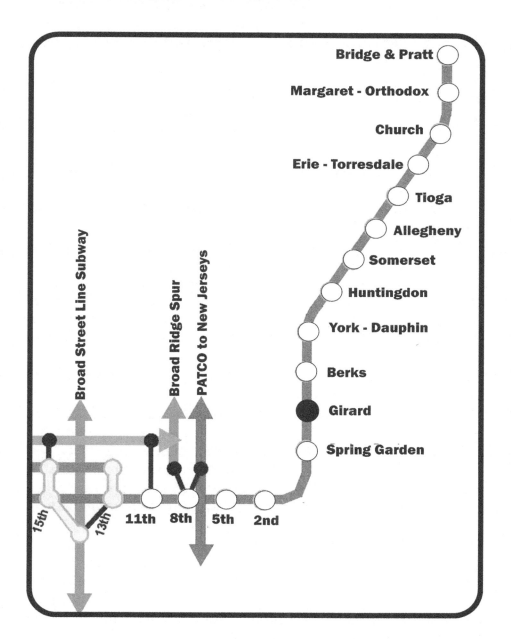

Girard

We called the guy, Jumpy Girard. What else would you call a guy who yelled out, "Girard" every day when the El was creeping into its Girard Avenue stop? Girard, the guy, didn't just say it once or twice. He made a chorus of it and it was his act. People had acts on the El rides, all kinds of stunts or looks, or moves. Some people did the dress thing, three-piece suits and brief cases for the top execs, although some with really simple jobs also carried that briefcase act to work. That's how the brass-snapped, leather briefcase with only a peanut butter and jelly sandwich and cookie inside got fashionable. Ladies had numerous acts, and they were real big on the looks or, "I'm not lookin" moves.

A girl we all knew and liked, once said to Danny, "I always got a kick out of how you pretended to be looking down my blouse when I was sitting on the El, Danny Fisher."

Danny, with that devil may care grin, told her, "I wasn't pretending."

Well, Girard, the guy, Jumpy Girard, was the last guy you would figure to do what he did. The train was stopped at the Girard Avenue Station. It was making that connection to the station platform, where everything gets kind of curious – you know, a huge machine stands still with its motors running and all the electric sounds and like a gaping monster it pauses with the doors all open. People seem like robots or toys in its presence. I don't think anybody was paying attention to Jumpy Girard, but when we thought about it later, Jumpy never said a word that morning.

Perfectly timed, Jumpy grabbed a pretty woman's pocketbook and pushed her over as he did. I will always remember seeing her falling backwards in shock. It was so odd to see her deep black hair spread out and touching the floor of the train. It was a premeditated act by Jumpy, because all he had to do was step back and he was out of the train door just as it closed. He was safe and would be long gone in a few seconds. I reached to help the lady, but Danny Fisher was moving like a sprinter off the starting block, and he came very close to catching Jumpy before the doors hissed closed on Danny's hand. The train was moving out of the station when it stopped and all the doors opened again. Danny was a flying dart across the plat-form and soon had Jumpy Girard tackled by the turnstiles. I caught up to them and crashed both my knees down on Jumpy's back.

Some guys on the station were ready to fight, but couldn't decide who to fight. There were cops there in minutes. Jumpy got cuffed and the woman got her pocketbook back, but she had to go to the hospital. Before you would imagine, we were back on the train, and moving fast again. It is always amazing how fast life on an El train returns to normal, like nothing happened, no matter what happened. The fast-acting El driver, they called, the Engineer, was the real cause of a good ending, but even he just got back in his compartment and moved the levers.

=/=/=/=/=/=

As we rode away from the robbery, it hit me that the woman who had been knocked over looked like somebody from the past. Finally I nudged Danny and asked.

"Did you help that woman because you knew her?"

"You're thinking of Rosie..."

"Yeah, Rosie what's her name?"

"Right, Pensabino."

"Gheez, yeah, Rosie Pensabino. She was your guardian angel or something when we were at the University. Did she really leave you money?"

"Some, yeah, not a lot, but I was her adopted child, in a lot of ways."

"That goes back, way back."

"I was seventeen when I fell in love with the thirty some year-old magnificent Italian Lady,"

That was back when your Dad, Lord rest his soul, screwed up her car in your old garage with the help of some of his crony friends, right?"

"Yep, Durk da Drunk and Chiclets."

"Rosie helped you to buy books and things when you won the full scholarship, didn't' she?"

"Yes, she did. I used to go nuts when she showed up on campus. She was so beautiful, and all woman."

"Do I remember that? We thought you were the wildest couple in Philadelphia. She loved you, man."

"Do you remember the story about all that? It was in the big folder I asked you to keep?"

"Now I do, funny stuff man, I had tears in my eyes reading and laughing at that episode in your young life. God, did we ever know how much damn good living and fun times we had as kids?

The Painters

A man with a corduroy jacket, forty-seven, sits on a bench in Philadelphia. He is Danny Fisher. He is bent over a letter and reading it a second time. He is remembering being seventeen and that time in his life is filling his mind as a scene three decades back, in a barroom manifests itself...

=/=/=/=/=/=

Danny, with his head down is listening to the male voices around him. Piled in compacted mounds or twisted and burst open, cigarette butts are everywhere. While he is staring at the designs in the floor tiles sloping to the front of the bar and rimmed by the brass rail, a man beside Danny bends his head down and spits.

Danny quickly moves his foot and faces away from the bar. He discovers Durkin's face in the long mirror on the wall in front of him. He notices the noise of glasses and coins behind him. Durkin's skin is gleaming from perspiration. It is a hot night in July. Durkin's curly hair is shiny black and matted to his head. He is smiling and talking, making his way through the crowd of men towards the back of the bar. The mirror is smeared and hand printed. At the same time that Danny sees his father's reflection, the, always intoxicated Chiclets walks past between Danny and the mirror.

Danny's eyes fill with smoke while he stares too long into the mirror. His head swollen with men's voices and his eyes stinging, Danny walks to the open front door appreciating the night outside as clean, hot and still. Danny sits on the tank of the air compressor his companions had left by the bar door earlier. Chiclets' brother had sold it to them. It is a paint sprayer, well used, maybe not worth what Danny's father, Durkin and Chiclets agreed to pay. They are going in the car painting business. Their first customer is the stylish, Italian woman with long black hair who always wears high heels and a silk scarf.

Danny often saw the woman sitting in the back room of the bar on Friday nights when he came to take home his father's pay. He is picturing Durkin in the back room of the bar with the Italian woman. He imagines her. She holds a cigarette like the femme fatale in those revealing shadows of film noir. She pauses after each drawn breath, smoky clouds form from her lips, fulfilled in lofty ascending and encircling forms.

The back part of the bar was always mysterious to Danny; most men stay out in the front. Danny always works up the courage it takes for him to pass through the back room from the bar's side entrance. The Italian woman will speak to him with either an affected romantic interest or her natural geniality. He likes her, often innocently responding to her sensuality, but sometimes deliberately.

Danny is seventeen; the woman, middle-aged, full breasted, shapely. He notices she always wears a skirt or dress. He cannot think of her without imagining her legs or hips. He has a habit of showing her his test marks from school while on his way to the front bar. She takes the always crumpled and folded papers and smiles approvingly at him while he pauses before her. After a few seconds of her attention, he rushes off to find his father in the male-filled front bar.

Danny hears the Italian woman laughing back in the alley beside the bar. He stands up and goes over to the alleyway noticing the blackness above the street lights and that only a few cars were on the avenue. Durkin is with her.

"Hi, Rosey," Danny offers.

"Danny! Hello, Sweetie, how's my handsome man. You gonna be one of the painters?"

He smiles sinking his hands into his pockets. She turns back to Durkin. Chiclets comes out of the front door and starts dragging the compressor across the sidewalk. His only two teeth are suspended in his smile, the cause of his nickname.

Durkin says, "We ain't goin' yet."

Chiclets stares at Durkin blankly while Danny's father appears in the doorway.

"All right, Chiclets," Durkin says. "I guess we're goin, the master painter is here, right, Rembrandt?"

Danny's father is staggering, his body drifting after each step. The woman reaches her hands up into her long black hair and gathers it at the back of her neck. She watches Chiclets and Danny's father struggle to put the compressor into the trunk of Durkin's gray Nash. Durkin and Danny both stare conspicuously at her breasts protruding beneath her raised arms. Durkin touches her elbow and Danny's interest melts into shyness when she looks at him and then Durkin. Durkin boldly smiles and says, "You don't get a free paint job every day now, do you, Rose?"

"No, Tom. My car is all faded, it needs it." She lets her hair fall out of her hands. Danny's eyes watch it with admiration, his gaze remaining as if it would go on and on, settling like falling feathers.

Durkin, dark and handsome in the yellow-orange streetlights, closes the trunk saying, "Well, mates, let's get the job done. The lady needs a fancy car for her Sunday drives."

"Think it'll be nice black, Tom?"

It was the first time Danny hears her call Durkin Tom, but he is enjoying her too much to be jealous. Durkin looks up and down the sidewalk pretending to see if anyone else was listening and says, "It'll look so good, Rose. You'll want me to paint your backside to match."

Danny is surprised to see the woman's pleasure with the description. He is hoping Durkin will say something like that again, something more vulgar. Danny's father clumsily guides Danny to the backdoor of Durkin's car. When the four painters are all in Durkin's old sedan, the woman leans into Durkin's open window giving him a quick kiss. Then she looks back at Danny and says, "You really gonna help 'em paint my little Chevy, Danny?"

"Sure he is," Durkin answers.

"Danny's gonna paint a bit," his father adds.

"We's in the paintin' business, right, Danny?" Chiclets said, slapping Danny's knee. Chiclets, as drunk as a man can be, is still conscious.

The woman steps backwards on the sidewalk waving. Danny thinks she is waving directly at him.

As they lurched away, she is standing in the light from the open bar door. Danny searches the light from the bar that silhouettes her legs beneath her skirt. Danny keeps seeing the excitement of her in his mind while the old sedan rides off to the wooden garage his father and Durkin had built before Danny was born.

The paint sprayer and compressor moves around in the trunk as they drive. There had been one great thud when they first pulled away from the bar. There was no concern from the others. Danny is busy daydreaming about how good it was to be doing something for the woman. He thinks she will surely make a fuss over the parts he paints.

When they pull up the driveway, Danny looks for the car in the darkness as if it was a part of the woman. It is hers and somehow it is she. He can't wait to work on it and make it please her. He imagines her touching the new paint with him and smiling with appreciation for him.

Chiclets has been snoring and Danny's father is coughing and spitting into a coarse brown paper towel. Danny remembers all their great plans about the car painting business and how they talked about it all week. Durkin had often said, "Nothing like a new paint job. We'll be racking in the dough."

Danny's father walks into the pitch-black garage finds the light bulb hanging from a rafter and turns it. The light is like a go signal to Danny. He gets out and rubs his hand along the full length of the woman's car. Reaching the front end, he turns expecting to see the others following.

His father is back behind Durkin's car opening a quart of beer. Durkin and Chiclets are still in the car. They are talking loud about Chiclets' brother. Danny is used to waiting for them to do things, but it is too annoying this time.

He walks away disgusted and goes into the old wooden framed house he and his father live in. He turns on the radio and walks to his father's night table and steals a cigarette. He picks up a paper that has his father's signature on it and brings it and the cigarette to his room. Folding the paper, he carefully places it in an envelope thick with other papers. He lays across his bed and lights up his father's cigarette thoughtfully breathing smoke into the air listening to the songs, one after another, coming from the kitchen. He is inhaling regularly now.

Smoking makes him feel older and more interesting. Smoking puts him in his favorite mood, thinking of the smoking and imagining what he seems to be to others; people that like him. He falls asleep after the second stolen cigarette. The thick envelope was under his pillow.

Hours later, his father wakes him.

"Danny, c'mon and see the car, c'mon!"

Danny is out walking across the stone driveway, his eyes fixed on the wet black shine on the woman's car. From outside of the garage it looks good under the garage light.

"Dad, where are Durk and Chiclets?"

"Chiclets' on the porch. Durk left. He was sick from the paint."

"Wow, it's thick."

"Yeah."

"And running. Still wet, gheez, Dad!"

"Did it good though, Cole."

"Whatta ya wanna do, Dad?"

"Damned if I know. It's done."

"You wanna just wipe it off?"

"Yeah, maybe some spots."

"What else could we do?"

"Get some good rags, if you want."

"T-shirts be best."

"OK. Ghaw ahead."

Danny runs for the bathroom and pulls three of his tee-shirts out of the wash basket. When he comes back, his father is sitting, almost asleep, on the big blank board seat he had built beside the garage where the rhubarb patch comes up every year.

Danny finds the thickest paint and most runs on the driver's door. The paint had obviously been flowing down the door like maple syrup. He opens a tee-shirt and rubs with both hands across the door.

The paint comes off easily. "At least the mess comes off," he says, perhaps loud enough for his father, but more for his own benefit.

Suddenly the woman comes into his mind and everything Danny does say or thinks is for her benefit. He works the whole car over, rubbing off excess paint and then spraying a thinner coat over the dullness the rubbing left. He notices the chrome and windows the others had failed to cover and how the paint seeped in under the tape and news-paper they had put on too loosely or carelessly to mask those parts not to be painted.

His father fills the spray bottle when it needs it, but otherwise stays in the dark out by the rhubarb. He speaks to Danny a few times but only with tired unconcern until finally he says,

"That's lookin better, Cole. You're a better painter than the rest of us."

"It works best when you don't get too close with the spray, see?"

"Ya, Danny, Jesus, it looks good enough. I think ya got it. Wanna wash your hands. There's some turpentine in the corner." Danny obeys and they go to bed.

Late the next morning Danny and his father are left alone when Durkin and Chiclets went off to the place they called "The Club." It is Sunday and "The Club" is the only place open that serves drinks.

Danny sits on a milk box staring at the car. It is still a mess. There are paint streaks he had missed and dull blotches where he had attempted to make the corrections. Lumps and beads of paint and dust particles are captured and fingerprints seem to be everywhere. In places, the tee-shirt left unmistakable marks like when you drag a soft broom across fresh fallen snow.

Danny is facing the car when the woman arrives. His father speaks to her first, "It's done." Danny saw that his father had no connection to the woman and none of her attention. Danny is mumbling, but his words are all too softly spoken to be understood. He is scraping his foot in the gravel and holding his head down. His father's hand sticks to the paint on the roof while he touches the car and says, "It won't rust up on ya, Roseanne, we got plenty of paint on her."

Again, as if she heard none of it, she touches the paint on the glass in the driver's door as if she has to confirm the sight of her car with her fingers. Her brown eyes open wide and glistening in the sunlight. Danny's father opens the door, rolls the paint, dabbled window down quickly, and shuts the door. The woman turns away and starts to walk back down the driveway. She hadn't said anything. Danny's father stands holding the car keys watching her leave.

Danny goes over and sits on the big blank board bench in front of the rhubarb patch. The woman comes back in about an hour with Durkin's wrist in her hand and Chiclets trailing behind.

She stands beside the worst part of the car, the driver's door, the calves of her legs stiffened above her high heels. She takes the keys abruptly from the outstretched hand of Danny's father only to find they stick to her fingers. Now thick, wet paint is on her. When she sweeps her hand through her hair from exasperation, strands of hair stick to her fingers.

Durkin walks around the whole car in a mannerism imitating an inspector. He stops at the door opposite Rose and laughs out loud. She angrily slaps the keys down on the hood of the car and walks down the driveway close to the rose bushes. Danny stands up and begins to follow her at a distance.

When she passes the rose arbor at the end of the driveway, she turns and walking in the sunlight down the middle of the street she draws Danny's feelings out of every part of his youthful heart. Her long black hair is more beautified by the sunlight. Danny looks through the rose arbor paralyzed with embarrassment. The shapes of her calves above her slender ankles instantly make him look more intently, tracing the skirted curves of the shape of her thighs. He is thrilled by her and watches her hips moving in the enraged expression of her energetic gait. Her femininity is heightened in the eyes of the seventeen-year-old. Danny's face grimaces with shame, his eyes finally locked in an expression of regret.

Durkin comes down the driveway and standing behind Danny he says, "She is smoking mad, Danny, hot tomato!"

After an undetectable gasp, Danny turns back to Durkin who curiously followed him down the driveway, "We treated her bad, Durk."

"We'll fix it, Danny."

"The car?"

"Yeah, kid."

"Maybe she won't want you to fix it. Maybe she's too angry for that."

"She'll get over it, Danny."

"I wish I hadn't touched it. Why's she mad at me?"

"That's women, Danny," says Durkin.

Danny looks at the middle-aged man for a long moment. Then he tears off a rose from the arbor. He runs into the house and to his bedroom and returns clutching the envelope from under his pillow and the rose. He trots down the street suddenly looking manly more perhaps than ever expected by him or his onlookers and yet every bit of seventeen years old. He is feeling newly discovered strength in the muscles of his legs and where he is centered in his heart and from the rhythmic breathing in his lungs.

Durkin bends forward through the arbor, in an over-muscled stance, almost falling forward, looking at the boy in disbelief. Danny moves with his newly achieved graceful, masculinity, carrying him and the envelope and his rose very deliberately forward until he reaches the middle-aged woman. He notices for the first time that he is taller than she. Danny first touches the rose to her hand noticing the delicate fabric of her skirt clinging to the paint on the back of her thumb. Then he gives her the envelope not saying a word.

Durkin, now at a distance, gulps in disbelief tasting beer in his throat and questioning momentarily when he had begun to drink so early in the mornings. He searches blindly for the memory of himself being seventeen.

He watches Danny and the woman walking together down where the road turns. She dangles the rose at her side in a motion like that when a woman places one leg over the other and sways her foot toward the object of her romantic attention.

Nearly out of Durkin's sight, the young man, feels wonderfully warm in the sunlight walking in the middle of the road with the Italian woman. She had opened his envelope and was reading the papers it contained.

Danny senses that Rosey is exquisitely perfumed. Everything is about her. She says, "You've been accepted to the University, Danny. It's your freedom, your own life's path. I'll help you a little if you need it. You can pay me back when you get rich and famous. I see your father signed, that's good, Danny. It's a grant and a scholarship. You can live on campus. I'll come to visit you there, Danny. I'll have to take the subway since my car looks like it melted. I knew all those good grades you got would mean something one day. You're my college man now, Danny Fisher."

She smells the rose affectionately and smiling with her tearful, brown, Italian eyes, she says. "Durkin told me you tried to fix my car for hours last night. I may not be as smart as you but I'm getting smarter. I think my next boyfriend will be the intelligent type, sounds fine. Tell one of those Professors about me, okay? I'm ready to give up painters and go for Professors. Think one of 'em would like me, Danny?"

"Maybe I'll be a Professor one day,

Danny Fisher, thirty years later, sitting on a wooden bench on a spring day along Locust Walk, folds a letter he received from a friend in his old neighborhood. It had said in the second paragraph that a Rose Pensabino had died from injuries sustained when struck by a bus in North Philadelphia in front of Sweeny's Tavern. She was very old, it said, and was hit crossing the avenue on a Saturday night.

He thought about how she would stand before the front door of Sweeny's and how the night sky is very dark above and beyond the street lights. The letter said, she had him in her will to receive some money and her jewelry and that she had no one else.

Inside the envelope he found a black and white photograph of an old car; a, Chevy Coupe with a paint job worse than he remembered but not without a certain glow and sparkle that maybe only Danny Fisher could see.

Spring Garden

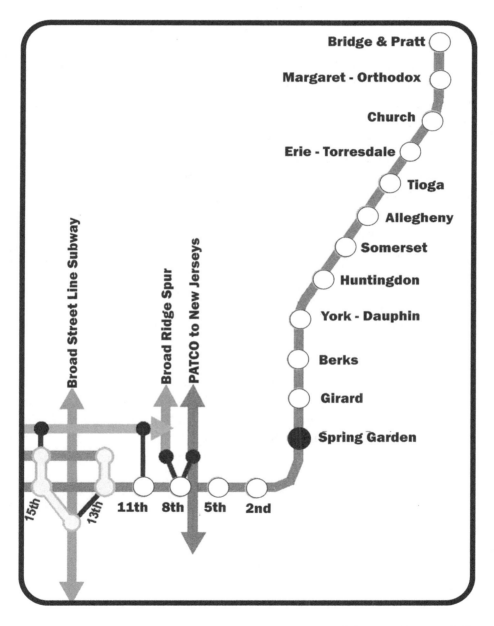

It was raining hard that day we passed through the Spring Garden El stop not engaged in any conversation. I was reading a book that day. It was a story about what guys carried in combat. Something about Spring Garden reminded me that Danny wasn't on the El train the day before. I didn't see him all that day. Then it came back to me, and I asked him,

"What happened when you went to the V.A.?

"Same shit. They never change."

"I never knew what happened to you in the army.

"Well, we weren't allowed to talk about it, Top Secret shit, man."

"Yeah, but that was years ago."

"Are you sure I never told you."

"I'd remember that, no way I'd forget that, Dan. What you told me here at Spring Garden two days ago won't ever be forgettable."

"Do you want to read my notes from my V.A. appointment yesterday?"

"Absolutely."

"You put that with an implied object. It didn't go that way. The V.A. is a nebulous experience, indefinable. I started going there when I first realized what I was faced with; nothing comes of it except bureaucratic crap. Hear read this..."

Any Day at the VA

Interior - Philadelphia V.A. Hospital - Mid-day - Present Time

Danny Fisher, standing with his hands in his pockets and his shoulders flexed forward expressing his determination to tell the story, begins speaking to a young nurse,

"When I was a boy they put us in a trench in some Godforsaken place in Nevada. I was a draftee and nineteen." He looked around to be sure no one else was listening.

"Look, first you gotta know I always tried to be a soldier for them. I believe the country is special and anyway, I never questioned that the army would treat me any different from any other citizen. I automatically trusted the army."

A navy nurse walked by and he stopped speaking. When she was out of earshot he continued, "I knew they might ask a lot of us or even expect us to die if we had to. It was the infantry. I always did what they told me. But I'll tell ya when I look back in history and the whole western world following those pompous cats in those horned helmets and full length overcoats strewn with ribbons and medals, the fuckin hats alone … Sorry… but those dumb hats should have tipped everyone that they were all lunatics. Did you ever see that Kaiser Wilhelm and that Austria-Hungary guy, totally over the top. The German high command all had a horn sticking out of their helmets. What was that?"

"I'm talking about 1917, and ten million men tearing each other apart in the trenches. Can you imagine living in a killing trench year after year? What did it mean to 'em to see the spring come again and again and still they killed each other because the horned helmet nuts told them to."

Two men in security guard uniforms got off the elevator and went out an exit door. McGrath was surprised to see the young nurse still paying attention to him. He said,

"You're polite for listening to my jazz."

The young nurse, curious about why he didn't want to be heard by others, said, "No, it's interesting and I can't imagine what happened out there to you guys. It's unbelievable. Go on."

"What I'm saying is, the First World War, them dudes in the hats, the ones with the horns or the plucked feathers, were maniacs. They had brass bands and flags and they gave out boots and the uniforms. The only dudes who should ever wear uniforms are guys selling ice cream. Anybody else should be made to walk around in hospital gowns til they are no longer a danger to themselves or anybody else. You know, like you do in mental wards."

"There are way too many uniforms coming here."

"Well, it was the trench thing you see? They believed if you had a trench and a fancy uniform you'll win the war. The trench we were put in was only half as deep as a man standing but they still believed in trenches, so we had to sit crouched on the ground to keep our heads lower than the surface of the desert. You did that instinctively. When it went off, I was gonna close my eyes but my hands became transparent and I could see the bones inside them. The bones were black. The light was so bright I couldn't see anything but the bones."

"That really scared me. And I knew immediately that this was not going to turn out well, that what they were doing was a real bad idea. I felt as I had been betrayed, How do you figure you'll be put in a trench like that? It was evil. At the same time, and this is no bull, I felt the presence of something; something invisible, protecting me."

His shallow breathing becomes audible. The young nurse looks at him sympathetically saying, "I have to go up and see what they want to do." She motions to him to sit and wait.

He watches the young nurse walking, his eyes following her to the elevators until the doors close. He looks around and focuses on the glass front door and reads the letters spelled backwards on the glass, Veterans Administration. The panicky feelings persist.

Breathing in controlled rhythm, he whispers, "Distractions, walk the beach … Walk the beach … Why do I come back here?" He sits down. "There's no help here. I feel the chemistry getting messed up again, calm down. It's… See the floss from dandelions in the wind … See the floss."

Before his mind could image what he wanted to see, he saw the desert and the atomic bomb exploding. In his place in a squad of infantry he is running. They are charging ground zero. At his feet there is a crackling crust of black moving over a lava flow. He has to leap across, he does but the heel of his combat boot sinks into the inferno. He leaps again running faster, exhausted and nearing heat stroke. The scene begins to repeat itself as it always does.

The young nurse is back in front of him, her eyes widening as she realizes his distracted condition, He reemerges for her benefit and because she is talking.

132

"You have to go to section H for blood work, Okay? Why were you guys exposed to atomic bombs? Did they eventually tell you why?"

"Dunno, they were all lunatics, crazy scientists and military cats."

"Yeah, I would say so. They know about you guys upstairs. I'm afraid it is all arranged...," she paused and drawing an audible breath she added, "They knew about it."

"Where is section H?"

"They close at four o'clock, Can you come back tomorrow?" she asked.

"Nah, one day is enough, thanks."

"But... I understand," she muttered her words with her head turned and eyes inviting him toward the exit-way out of the hospital.

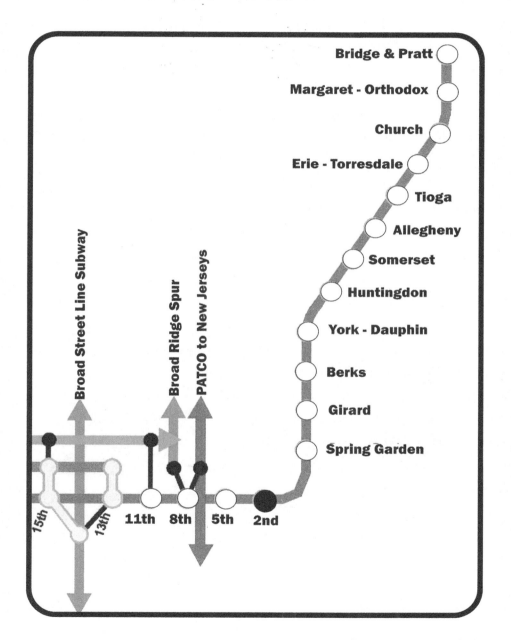

Chapter 13

Danny Fisher won a Literary Award for this Philadelphia Story. He told me that when he first turned the story in, the Newspaper Editor, an old reporter named Scoop, of course, told Danny he was going to do him a favor and keep the manuscript in his desk drawer and never publish it. He warned Danny that some city guys might want to rough him up about the content.

Sidewalk Sanctification

On Broad Street in the Philadelphia Mummers Parade

Tyson Tucker's white shoes now matched the gray snow along the curbs. They were soaked through to his socks from stepping in and out of the flow of gutter water. His shoulder up near the nape of his neck pained him. Looking ahead, he could see the end of the parade and buses parked and their motors sending plumes of exhaust into the winter air.

The music was spirited as it always was during the last song. Tucker couldn't remember the bridge, so he held his pick loose, smiled thinly, and faked it, joining in again reluctantly when the second chorus started. After the song, the music director's whistle blew, and in what looked to be one motion, the bandsmen all quit the parade stride. Tucker had stopped in place at the whistle, hoisting his banjo strap angrily over his head to relieve his sore neck. Dockstader's kid came up and handed him a can of beer. They walked together splashing through the gutter water once more before stepping up on the sidewalk.

"Good parade, T.T., huh?"

"Ah, it's a tank town, Low Dock."

Dockstader, the kid's father, was by far the tallest man in the band, His son was probably the shortest. The kid was nicknamed "Low Dock" during the joking on the bus that morning.

"What's a tank town, Tuck? Whatta ya mean?"

"Hey, kid, there's only one parade. Damn slush!"

Tucker was examining the wet dirt on his trouser cuffs.

"Oh yeah?"

"Yeah, all this other stuff's just jobs. Ya know?"

"Guess so, haven't been there yet."

"Oh, yeah, you ain't been down the street yet."

Tucker faced away from the kid and scented out his banjo case in the pile of band equipment beside the bus. Bending down to put the instrument away, he said, "What the hell's your first name anyway?"

"Jules."

"What's that, a Jew name?"

The kid's eyes opened wider matching a sudden flare in his nostrils. "Jewish? I don't know, maybe it's German, but my . . ."

"Whatever. Aren't you gonna play?"

137

"Soon as they give me a suit."

"You don't need a damn suit. Look kid, it's the only way you learn is to play. It's not easy to march and play, like chewing gum and walking."

"Yeah, I guess you get all messed up, don't yuh?"

"Is the Pope Catholic? You'll think you can't do it, but, if you try instead of waitin' for a damn suit, you'll get it. You'll be ready, maybe."

Tucker opened another can of beer. The kid noticed the whole band was around them. Among those listening, some appeared interested others seemed pleased to show they had heard it all before. The kid felt embarrassed after Tucker's criticism.

After the bus was on its way, the kid deliberately displayed his first can of beer. Tucker saw it.

"Hey, kid, Jules," Tucker said grinning, "is this, your banjo up here, kid?"

"Yeah, T.T."

"Let's see it."

"Ghaw ahead."

Tucker took down the banjo, strutted up the aisle with it, and coaxed Lafferty, the base fiddle player, into getting his instrument from the back seat. In a minute they finished off their cans of beer, tuned, and started plucking. The music, the singing, and the rhythm of the bus, were hypnotic to the kid. Twisted around in his seat, he followed Tucker's hands, the one racing up and down the banjo neck; the other flailing rhythms. He looked beyond Tucker's hands, mouths in laughter and faces strained in song.

"That banjo never sounded like that before!" he thought. "Tucker's something else."

The kid felt happy among the busload of men where comedy was king and music the perfect excuse to be together.

"I'm gonna play next time. Tucker's right. Ya gotta just do it. I'll do it."

The kid sat back in comfort. It was dark outside when the bus hissed to a stop. After the costumes and instruments were unloaded, the kid carried Tucker's headpiece and walked beside him. Their steps crunched into the soft spring snow. The sound of the bus was dying in the distance. Tucker spoke, sending breaths smelling of beer into the damp night air. He had been noticing the simplicity of willingness in the boy's ways and now it bounced in the kid's walk.

"That's a good banjo ya got there, kid. It's got a nice ring."

"Thanks. I can't wait to play with you guys on the next job."

"You know what, kid? You're gonna be dynamite! I can tell."

The kid slowed, changed his grip, and then hastened to catch up to the older bandsmen.

=/=/=/=/=/=

It was the seventh concert in the park; the last one before the bandstand closed. The temperature had dropped down that night and a breeze blew in under the metal canopy bringing with it a waterfront chill. The summer was over; the kid's first summer with the band. Together, they played the slow part of a medley of big band favorites. The audience was in a lull with the sound and the kid's eyes were scanning the seated horseshoe shape of the band. He fixed a stare on the distorted shape of Tucker's nose pressed against the neck of his banjo. Two elderly couples danced on the blacktop parking lot over Tucker's shoulder.

Tucker wasn't playing; he looked angry. The kid became disturbed by Tucker's blatant lack of showmanship. Finally, Tucker began to play, but his eyes held a contemptuous expression until they finally shut in concentration and opened in the warm languidness of the music. Wondering why Tucker had been angry, the kid went back to watching the audience. He focused on an apparently retarded girl dancing without a partner. In the moment, she captured his attention.

"She's . . . oh, that's it."

He looked over at the elderly black couples dancing on their make-believe ballroom confirming his suspicions about Tucker's behavior.

=/=/=/=/=/=

When the concert was over, the group that always lingered was standing on the gravel road that led down to a boat launch. Everything was dark out on the river except the lights from the ferry. Sounds of laughter and voices seemed to hang back in the air over the water as if the boat taking away the audience couldn't pull hard enough to break their previous attachment to the shore.

The bandsmen made shuffling noises in the gravel and their presence there launched the smell of beer and burning tobacco out after the ferry. Tucker looked out towards the people on the river and said, "Don'tcha hate playin' for a bunch of blacks? Cept we show 'em every time that a white man's got as much rhythm as any of 'em ever dreamed of."

Some of the others looked out towards the sounds on the ferry. The kid looking down at the gravel said, "Are you serious, Tucker?"

Then he lifted his head and stared out into the dark over the river and said, "What the hell ya gettin' all angry about those people for?"

Lafferty, standing behind Tucker, stepped forward and said, "The Jew kid likes spooks, Tuck."

"Shut up, Lafferty!" Tucker growled.

The kid started walking away, noticing Lafferty's scowl as he passed him. Tucker pretended to be yelling something insulting and racial out at the ferry in a pantomime-strained voice with hands cupped at his mouth. The others, including Lafferty, laughed in amusement. Then Tucker ran after the kid saying, "Hey, kid! Yo, kid, wait."

Catching up, he put his hand on the kid's shoulder and said, "Look, it don't mean nothin' to me."

"Humph, thanks!"

"No, kid. I don't care, really."

"What about what you just said about the blacks?"

"These bands like ours, even the East Side Band, they don't like blacks."

"That's pure crap, too."

"That's the way it is."

"Get outta here, Tucker. You can't tell me that even half the guys in this band would give a shit."

"C'mon back, kid. We're gonna play down at the Trap."

"Ah, I don't feel like it. We closed the Beast's bar last night. I'm checkin' out, T.T."

"Ya, all right."

=/=/=/=/=/=

The kid was pleased with himself in his sequined and boa feather-trimmed bandsman costume with its gold brocade, blue satins and jewel-like reflections from little round mirrors, cerise lace, and long, white ostrich plumes. It was the day of the parade that Tucker had spoken to him about back on that first bus job.

Directly beside the band in the street and above the crowds on the sidewalk, a priest stood on the steps of his South Philadelphia church. He was preparing to bless the band, the fourteenth to pass him that day. Both Tucker and the kid watched and heard, "God, Our Father, your gift of water brings life and freshness of the earth. It washes away our sins and . . ." The music started abruptly among cheers and a sudden smile from the priest who had begun to fling his holy water into the air.

The band had started marching to an old tune, popular in the twenties. Its crescendos and simple charm sent the great parade's gaiety into the kid and he swung with each step as he strummed the banjo strapped across his chest.

Tucker's account of the racial history of the bands came into his mind as they began marching out of the white ethnic neighborhoods of the city. Somewhere in the inner-city slum, he felt tightened about it all. The streets were lined with blacks, mostly whole families sitting on lawn chairs or standing with their kids who lined the curbs. The kid was on the end of a row, right beside the crowds. The band stopped at a street corner. The people there were almost silently gazing at the costumed musicians the way vacuous spectators do when they know a marching band has been caught in a parade delay. The crowd relaxed, talking to each other.

To the kid, the all-white band suddenly seemed to be a separate being, a bizarre feathery form unattached to the streets or curbs, majestic passing sprites cruelly indifferent to the people on the sidewalks. In the corner of his eye, he saw other bandsmen's long, gentle African ostrich plumes disinterestedly touching brown hands, winter clothing, children's shoulders and unfolded chairs.

The kid panicked, thinking, "They think I'm prejudiced against 'em just because I'm in this band. What a lousy mess I got myself into with this."

The kid, his face expressing his self-reproach, looked at the black children on the edge of the curb in front of their parents and neighbors.

"They could just assume I'm some kind of white bigot nut." The kid's face expressed his pain and confusion. "Who's really prejudiced? How many of these guys?"

Names darted in and out of his mind until he settled on a few he assumed to be clearly against the blacks. His grief heightened.

After a brief trance, he thought, "Hey, there's a lot of nice people in this band. They can't all be haters. There's some nice to everybody. Darn it all! We got the biggest chance in the world! We oughta . . ."

Everyone near him started reacting to the parade moving again. Tucker and the others were yelling out the song they would step out on. The black people were stirred by it. The kid was relieved by their smiles. He faced the crowd and said aloud, "Happy New Year," breaking the long silence between the two groups.

The kid turned back, embarrassed and awkwardly preparing to play and step off. He noticed a man's brown hand at his side. The kid took hold of the hand, looking at the gesture of the handshake appreciatively. He started marching and found he was out of step with the band and fumbling for the right chord. The song was easy and happy and he picked up the step quickly. The people on the sidewalk were all standing up now, some dancing, some clapping and shouting out praises. The kid smiled and looked for the faces that would see his. He stepped with a swinging motion to the music. He saw Tucker pulling up his banjo and indicating a pain high on his shoulder by the nape of his neck under the banjo strap.

The kid was enjoying the band's volume, his own music meshed into the total sound, his own rhythms beginning somewhere in the magic of it all. He noticed Tucker wasn't playing. The people on the sidewalks were celebrating. The kid caught Tucker's attention and sternly motioned him to play. Tucker understood but it had unexpectedly begun to rain large shockingly cold drops at first then a sudden downpour. Like an unwound toy, the band stopped playing and stood still in the street.

While the streetlights went on over the halted band, the black people, whole families moving backwards, offered protection to the bandsmen. They were calling them under sidewalk trees and the over-hanging parts of buildings. The lights shined, glistening on their faces showing concern and laughter.

Tucker shouted, "Balls on a bunch of rain, play! All right, kid?"

Someone in the crowd yelled, "Band's got heart! Rain or shine!"

The band formed in the street again in the pouring rain. The drum-beat started. The music director shouted. The music began. The crowd stayed, filled with the force of its own pleasure. The kid and Tucker stood side-by-side, rain falling on their faces, playing to the crowd.

When the band marched away, the rain, swept in a sudden strong wind, washed over the empty street behind them. Tucker smiled know-ing the kid had discovered both merriment and remorse. Tucker also knew instinctively that the kid might never march the big parade again. Tucker had seen that kind of shame before.

When the song was over and only the drummers' sticks kept time on the metal drum rims, Tucker, wiping rain off his face, dealt with another inner frustration. The pain up in the nape of his neck had started again. He whispered in hissing disgust, "I've gotta quit this freakin' band . . . another damn year . . . damn! I always feel this way . . . always wanna quit it . . . never do."

The kid began to feel water dripping on his hair. It was leaking through his headpiece. The events of the day and other times he had spent in the band collected in his mind in carefully connected fragments until he saw them as one body. Soon nothing was left to think of but himself and the rain, the dripping on his hair, and the peace of clearly knowing what to do.

This story by John McCabe won the Short Story Conference Book Award from Bucks County Community College

Ringing in the New Year
WITH THE
PHILADELPHIA
MUMMERS'
STRING BANDS

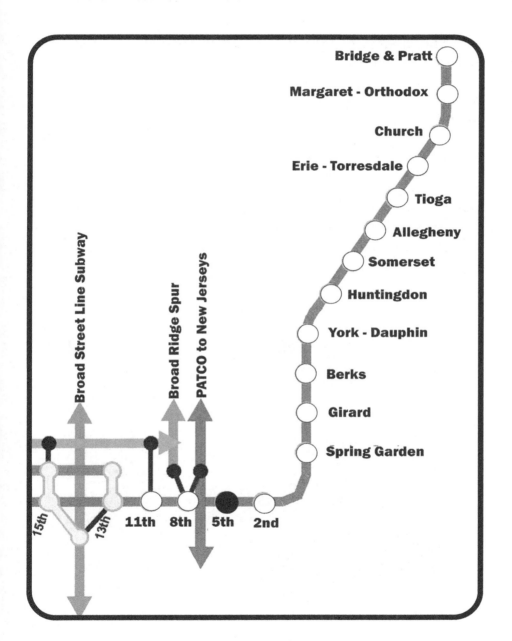

Chapter 14

5th Street in Philadelphia is no Fifth Avenue, New York, even though it has the same street number.

Danny always promised you could find the same kind of strap-hanging El Train riders in any other big cities, and you would feel the same there, the same unconnected connects.

"You would be with the daily commuters, among the people, so to speak, our people," he said.

Danny, when he became a syndicated writer, rode the trains in Chicago, Tokyo and London and, of course, New York. He had a story about a guy in Manhattan and a strange girl in the South Bronx. The guy was a priest and the girl was his girlfriend. Danny said the New York El train helped the story reach resolution. Danny and Bridget loved going to New York to do stories.

The Mission in the South Bronx

My name is Jeremiah Hopper. I'm a priest. As I said, I went back to the South Bronx today. I guess like all priests now, I am questioning everything, especially the fact that I had a girlfriend almost all my life, and the same girl.

I left the South Bronx when I was still a boy, to answer an ad for the foreign missions. I am probably the only priest in the Order who has never set foot on foreign soil. I was institutionalized at twenty-nine when first ordained. I have lived in and out of mental wards most of my life. I have always been a willing patient sometimes even admitting and releasing myself from their care.

My residence is near 60th and Tenth Avenue, in Manhattan. The Order has always let me keep my own room behind the novitiate house. I offer daily Mass at 6:30 A.M. to no more than ten individuals, not many when you consider the population around what used to be called, Hell's Kitchen. Oh, and I do kitchen prep work, peeling carrots and potatoes, making salads, and baking bread. I do simple maintenance jobs, and I am one of the Chaplains at the hospital on 10th when they call me, mostly on the weekends, of course. I occasionally have to do spiritual counseling work for mental patients, if they contact me. Well, that is pretty much my life, but this is what happened today when I was invited to walk in the garden, when I went back to the South Bronx because of Clare.

Some of the patient-residents sat under the ancient oaks in the garden behind that nineteenth-century, three-storied Victorian on Corinthian Avenue. Others walked around what appeared to be the maximum perimeter accessible to them. As much as they were individuals and centered as such, they were also a community. One woman was dancing on the grass with an invisible partner. I noticed others staring at me while the dancer gave me a faint wistful smile mostly in her eyes, the expression also traced into her heavily powdered face. My feelings about makeup being a deception surfaced but, even though her eyebrows were painted-on and not exactly in the right places, her smile appeared to be unmistakably genuine.

The looks that Clare was capable of creating were remarkable. Nobody knew about Clare and me except some old people who knew us when we were very young. I became conscious of minute but unexpected tremors in my senses. I turned and finding a lawn chair, I sat down and I thought,

"Yes, I remember being intrigued that first time when I first met Clare when she gazed at me through the back window of a car parked on Emlin Street, right here in the South Bronx near the Cloistered Monastery."

Some of the residents were whispering to each other. I couldn't make out what they were saying. I was taken aback by their respectful attention toward me. In my mind, I began again, "I remember you, Clare," I thought, "and how you looked at me as if I were your prophet, a poet to send you verses about everything you would ever care about as long as you lived." I looked up into the tall trees. "How did that glance, the look from the back seat of that car, manage to last so long? Always, I am able to recall it with the same private drama. How could it still be there, suspended in my memory?"

Maybe the administrator wanted me to tell her my thoughts about Clare. If she asked or made it more obvious, I would have talked to her. I wondered how much she already knew. She said Clare's name so ruefully.

"I always loved your name. Clare. It..." The woman dancing gesturing with her eyes and moving her lips interrupted me with a wave of her hand. She wanted to speak. I turned toward her. She bent down and touched her knees with both her hands and speaking softly said, "Clare," that was all. I was looking up from her dimpled knees when her eyes met mine.

"Yes," I said, wondering how she knew. All the people in the garden seemed to know why I was there. The way she touched her knees was familiar to me, for some reason. She looked over, prompting me to go on speaking. Then I remembered Clare would do the same thing sometimes just bending over and touching her knees. I was impressed by the dancer's genuine interest. "She wouldn't be a good listener," I thought. I smiled and walked over to another sitting area and I slid back into a lawn chair, stretching my feet out for comfort.

The dancer also sat in one of the chairs. I noticed her also relaxing. Two other women walked by they were younger and very talkative, one cursed a lot and the other agreed with everything that the cursing woman said. I looked up through the oaks and hemlocks again. It was midday. It was as if everything was coming to a stop. Life was going to pause at last.

I was waiting for Catherine Farrell, the administrator. The administrator was who I wanted for company, what I needed. The dancer smiled with a convincing sanity in her expression. I thought, "Who knows how sane or insane anyone is." Another sensation, this time, embarrassment was forming and my face felt hot. I shuffled my feet and followed other patient's actions with my eyes innocently showing my distress and alerting those around me. It was controlling to have them to look at because they were all so interesting but I needed to not fit in. The dancer kept one shoe moving scrapping the ground softly, her dance.

A bright red cardinal suddenly perched on a branch right in front of the dancer woman and me. The red bird began its repetitive chirping as I began to motion to the woman to look at the cardinal. Then as the administrator appeared and sat down with the dancer woman and me on my side of where the cardinal had been chirping, the dancer got up and walked off. I thought she was mimicking the cardinal's flight.

As the administrator Catherine Farrell spoke to me again about Clare, I realized I remembered her and that I knew her. She lived on Clare's block off of Lafayette when we were children. The woman knew and looked as if she was expecting my grief. She saw the tearing in my eyes.

"Clare so loved the flowers," I said, sobbing. Catherine Farrell sat up a bit. Her ribbon blouse flashed a jeweled pin in the sunlight magnified by my tears and I blinked wanting to shut my eyes. She touched my arm and whispered, "If you wish, Jeremiah, I would like to tell you about you and Clare the way she told it to me. We were like sisters; the best of friends and you were her Prince. Would it comfort you to hear how she spoke about you to me? She never mentioned your priesthood."

It was hard for me to talk, but I nodded knowing nothing would comfort me more. Barely able to speak, I said, "I didn't remember you at first, I'm sorry."

"I'm Catherine, I think you were in my brother's class," she answered.

"No, he was older. I remember your whole family, go ahead please," I said, gulping breaths.

At times, while she was speaking to me, I was able to close my eyes and drink in the mental pictures of Clare and me that she was revealing. I saw much of my youth going by in her many accounts of the past.

After she told me all she remembered, she asked, "Now, please, Jeremiah, tell me what really happened all those years ago? Clare's illness was controlled for long periods when the medications worked. Why did your paths part, taking each of you in a different direction?

149

How come she never talked about you being a priest? I know I'm being a busybody, but we were the best of friends. I loved her."

I had been locked into her words and the wonderful expressions that came and went on her face. The woman would show me complete delight, and I would see a veil of youth appear on her countenance. Then when ruefulness would cover her being, reflecting Clare's feelings, her face carried that to me as well.

As she began to cease repeating Clare's soliloquies, silent moments were interspersed between us. I saw myself as a very young boy and the grocery store delivery bike I rode. I pictured myself, and how I always entered the garden by the rearmost gate and peddling right past the very place where we were sitting. I would have never thought, back then, of returning here at my age, and never dreamed of Clare being a resident of this place, God, no, never!

The administrator had posed questions, questions I could not avoid. She was patiently awaiting my reply. She knows I am preparing, struggling actually, to tell her some buried memory. It was undeniably true everything had come to a stop, my life, in time, was no longer advancing or retreating.

I was still, and so was Catherine Farrell. After all, I thought, "What more was there for either of us to understand?" I wondered how I could explain to her that I left Clare to keep her with me. It was always clear to me. If I had stayed we would have parted… She won't understand that.

"Catherine," I said, studying her curious, hazel eyes and with everything around us moving again, but slowly, still out of time, a blotch of sunlight moved over Catherine's chair and her face. She held her hand up to her eyes. The world is still in motion, I thought. A breeze stirred the heights of the great trees. She seemed to be listening to the leaves but her gaze never left my face, encouraging my words and the meanings behind them. I felt as if I were one of the trees and my words, the leaves in the wind. She was listening to our sounds with the same interest, the same welcomed ease. "Maybe I'm losing it again…," That scary thought crossed my mind.

I moved my one foot, pointing it toward her, and wanting to speak, but I heard the unceremonious, yet always sacred metallic knock of the Monastery bell.

"Oh, I remember that sound," I blurted.

"We still hear it every day."

As the bell tolled, I felt a kinship with the cloistered; their peace was temporarily mine. Then I began to speak, "Clare and I had issues to deal with as children. She had hers and I had mine. My father was a drunk and my mother an angry, cold woman...I suffered in their company; they were always fighting and breaking things like dishes, and things that meant something to someone, like a toy or a gift or even a door or window. The smashes were loud and alarming; I would wake in the morning to those sounds... Once I saw my mother fly back over a chair into a corner of the room."

Catherine Farrell winced in sympathy, "I didn't know..." she whispered.

"I am afraid they broke me also, and every once in a while, in my life, I break down again. My fragility was born in the unwarranted intensity and violence of my home, and particularly in the betrayals of trust, of which I was acutely sensitive. After my childhood, mean or angry people, or those who I even suspected might betray me, could devastate my balance... Later in life, my principal reaction, if I even suspected betrayal, was retreat."

"Was this why you didn't stay with Clare?"

"No. At first, yes, but not later in our lives, it was only part of what we experienced and it's true that I always wanted to go to foreign lands, distant and intriguing places... but that was also because of Clare."

"I would guess a lot was because of Clare." She paused and said, "I know how she could... get to know someone's inner being," speaking hesitantly while bowing her head down as if she might have overstepped a boundary.

Catherine Farrell looked up into the trees frowning in a questioning expression but we sat in silence for a few moments.

I noticed the sun was still in its midday orbit and that a streak of its illumination was sent as a stream of light into the garden behind one of the great oaks where the rhododendron and mountain laurels owned the landscape. The whole scene was very unusual in the South Bronx. The ray of light invited my gaze to its place off in the garden's otherwise cool and shaded area.

"Clare suffered in the neighborhood, didn't she, Father?"

"Let me think," I said, standing before the administrator's staring. "Just give me a moment, please."

She smiled faintly and shook her head in agreement. Her face held that concerned expression that she used when telling certain parts of Clare's story. She knew everything; all those things whispered in my ears years long ago, done by the viper types. I realized now, Clare had told all that inexplicable evil to Catherine Farrell, and how the acts of others were cruelly intentioned.

I said, "Clare was always different and a stunning beauty with a remarkable intellect that evoked jealousies and envious rumors and cutting remarks by those cowardly enemies to her private struggle for happiness. Other girls back then couldn't deal with her except to deride her especially to boys interested in Clare. There are those so proud they steal from the graces and pains of others to cover their own inherent weakness and insipid lives."

Trying to satisfy and respond to the administrator, another thought filled my mind. I asked, "Would you like to hear a poem I wrote about us back then? I think I remember my words. It was a long time ago."

"Yes, of course, I would. What was your poem, Jeremiah?"

"I forget the title, Oh no, I remember, it was "The Witness of Torment." I was always writing poetry because she brought out that spirit in me. I wrote some sweet things about her when we were children. I…"

"She told me you were a true poet."

"Well, I couldn't find ways to express my feelings otherwise but it was all just my own stuff, not like a real poet."

"Let me hear it, please."

I started the poem, remembering every line. Nearing the end of the poem, I lowered my voice to a whisper with a knot in my throat. Finished the verses, I turned away, embarrassed by the juvenile attempt at poetry, but she was kind and said nothing to further my shame. I was deeply pleased to have someone to tell my story to, someone who would only be interested in what happened not so judgmental of my priesthood, and the few experiences I had with the nearly ordinary and the romantic.

"Look, that may seem melodramatic to you but I wasn't always a priest. I always needed the poetry to say things. I guess it is like somebody who listens to the lyrics of songs to borrow feelings to match their own. I want to take a little walk. Will you wait for me?"

"Yes, I will be right here."

I walked off a few steps then turned back facing her, and said shyly, "Just so you know not all the poems were so heart-wrenching."

She had, what I was noticing to be, the look on her face that said, you didn't answer my questions.

"I knew she couldn't think of me as a priest for some reason." I blurted shamefully, "You know her father abused her when she was very little, and that is why later in her life she probably used her sexuality to excuse or to cover-up what the past otherwise concealed. If it got her

152

a boyfriend and pleasure for them both, then it was needed by her and acceptable in a sad way. It was part of her version of reality and her madness."

"I am baffled about her not telling us about you being a priest..."

"It was the conflicted part of her. To us, Catherine and to me, the boy off to nowhere in the foreign missions, I was never a priest to her and to me she was never crazy."

If I kept talking I thought I would break down in tears again. I said, "I want to go back to the gate I used to enter when I was a kid, Okay?"

"Okay," she said, while closing her eyes and nodding her head slowly just before acknowledging a frantic patient who needed her for something. When she fully engaged the patient, others came near to her and began to command more of her attention. One man was spitting on his own shoes and she got up and talked to him from his side.

I continued to walk away. A short barrel-chested man rushed up to me and asked, "Who died, Father? I shouldn't be in here and neither should you. The sleeping pills will kill you."

I shrugged my shoulders reaching in my pocket I fingered my packet of medications and said nothing to the man. He did a surprising move like a very imperfect somersault. I walked off stepping on pulled flowers he had strewn on the walkway.

The gate area was surrounded by blooming roses and a stand of lilies, fading stargazers and white bridal wreath bushes. I touched the bars and the iron locks on the gate and looked out at the old neighborhood. With my forehead pressed against one of the openings, I could see down the hill to the Avenues and where the main streets of the neighborhood came together. The buildings along the avenues all held memories, but none more prominent than the old South Bronx Movie Theater.

While I was still standing by the gate, the Monastery bell rang out the hour. The sound swept me back in time. I saw Clare and me walking from the theater in the pouring rain. It was our first date. Both of us were soaking wet, we walked in puddles and over beds of crimson and golden and brown fallen leaves strewn beneath the magnificence of those autumn trees. All the splendor of fall and the rain, caught in the streetlights, surrounded us. She was a match, in beauty, to everything in nature, and all that sidewalk lighting could present.

We walked side-by-side in that torrent of rain. When she turned to me, I could see her lips, moist, and red in an alluring contrast to the colors of fall around us. Her eyes, beyond any painter's skill, were almost transparent views to her giving soul. With her blouse rain-soaked and

153

clinging to her, I saw the natural sculpture of her breast. That was the only time we empowered ourselves to be completed, without any limitations perhaps because we stayed out in the rain together, the only people out on the sidewalks. Embracing each other was like two becoming one by warmth. Once again, she was living within the grasping efforts in my mind.

I knew there was no explanation for death -- no finality among spirits and the souls of spirits. I walked back and found the dancing woman sleeping, her face shaded by the wide brim of her faded purple bonnet. She slept as only the medicated do, as if dead. Catherine Farrell was gone, probably back inside the old mansion busied, no doubt, by the pressing responsibilities of her work.

I found my way out past the security desk and along the arbor-covered walkway to the front of the grand Victorian masterpiece. The front of the house was unfamiliar to me as a child. When I reached the cobblestone street, I kept walking, not wanting to turn around.

Everything I needed to understand and know was within me now. I had thought of it all in that garden and said things I never spoke of before. I walked down Lafayette Street past the Monastery, to take the elevated back to Manhattan. When I arrived at the corner where the El station was, I began my usual confusing and reproachful thoughts about Clare. My recent bout with a chronic illness and the gripping and daunting sad truth about her had kept me from Clare once again and sadly from her before her unforeseen death.

I knew her in life, and now in her death, but I don't know if Clare did, that we were the victims of irrational damage, and, yes, gossips and the shallow waters of our own challenged minds. We were in youth, too innocent and vulnerable to defend or understand ourselves. The greatest handicap to mental illness happens in the times you don't know that you are sick.

When I started climbing the stairs to the El station, with its cage-like steel fencing and three concrete landings to break the sixty-foot climb, I looked back over the South Bronx. It was busy, busier than ever, with industry and train tracks and factories. Below our old hilly residential streets, the sounds of truck traffic to and from Hunt's Point was incessant. Nevertheless, my childhood jumped out at me in the unforgettable voices of Clare's past. Those voices like that of the administrator whom I left as she became too busy were now my history.

When I made my exit of the mansion, I was escaping the ringing evidence of Clare's lifelong mental condition still trapped in that garden of psychiatric disorders once Castor's mansion. The crazy times which were probably caused by a genetic influence and that horrific childhood abuse managed to drive me off again. Remembering Clare's delusional times assailed my peace again with a sword-like cutting edge. My always subtle and cautious investigations turned up repeated and undeniable disclosures. Every village carries its history and a neighborhood is a true village. Catherine Farrell was another spokesperson for the strangeness and inexplicable injustices of the past.

Before I knew Clare, as young as she was, she had a condition like schizophrenia. While I was her boyfriend, she was being treated unbeknown to me. When we met again, and even those decades later as aging white-haired souls, she was still mysteriously affected by her disorder. She had always washed it all out of her mind in strange denials. I sadly confirmed that my old neurotic fears of Clare's possible betrayal were based on my youthful but insightful instincts of being overwhelmed by something about her. Finally, I gave in to my doubts and, blaming myself, when I was nineteen; I left her behind and the South Bronx and went to join the Missions.

There was, in the nature of her illness, a power that became a barrier and rendered an important part of her inaccessible and ultimately kept me from her complete self. Nothing was more alluring however than when she would be still and quiet and permitted me to gaze on her. I would just look at her face and her eyes and I was hypnotized. I was, from my damaged youth, a wounded being with illogical fears and persistent confusions.

The toughest human malady to deal with is found in the realms of our minds. She said we were so much alike we never argued and we were so familiar that our absences were always quickly erased. In the end, even in the grace of maturity, we were still conquerable because of the power of the dual or multiple personality. I have my times where I am another being, crippled by voices and obsessive thinking. We did truly connect, however, initially and especially in her temporarily unaffected and miraculous childhood love for me. No mental disease has the power to completely or consistently mask the real identity of the stricken.

I worked, since I was nineteen as a live-in, mentally-challenged priest in the shadows of high rise buildings on the Westside. No one knows this, at least I am convinced they didn't know, but Clare would come and secretly stay with me on days when she could, and some weekends from time to time. The times of her visiting were often interrupted by her knowing when the illness was coming on, and that she would need help. She would reveal her delusions to me as if only I could understand. Voices, she said, would interrupt her and she would leave asking me to walk her to her stop.

Different states of health permitted us to spend good days together. As far as I knew she never had anything permanently with a man. We remained friends, almost lovers, even though the long absences. Some of the separations, lasting years, caused us to nearly stop thinking about each other.

She hopelessly betrayed us many times way back when we were very young. As strange as it all was, I knew her ways, and that she had an inexplicable agenda that was hidden and complex. She had deep, intensely expressed, precipitously timed romances, with obviously care-fully pre-selected choices, with otherwise senseless results. When she tried to make love to me, I couldn't be sure whom of her personalities she was presenting.

I was rendered incapable of moving on, and a good candidate for the priesthood. It was what would have been a compelling clinical study of male/female behavior, fit for a textbook. Somehow sex was always separated from the unfathomable relationship with her that lasted a lifetime. Nothing she did was any odder than my own compulsions. In my bad times, I would sit by the Merry-Go–Round in Central Park, in rain and snow or sweltering heat, convinced that it was the only place in the world besides my early morning, all but unattended, daily masses, where I would not go mad. I think hers was also a revolving ride.

Once she said ours was the marriage of the mentally ill. My one-room dwelling was our place. The church on 59th was where we stood in the back while a young couple was getting married. She repeated their vows to me, whispering the words. Clare said, "I borrowed their wedding."

We did things that normal people did at the times when we were both coincidently, sane personalities. The rest of our times belonged to the doctors, the pills and the dimly lit rooms and silent ceilings. For me, the priesthood, peeling carrots or fixing a light switch or just sweeping off the front steps on 10th street in Manhattan, was my therapy, alone hardly ever idle, but idle or busy, occasionally crazy as hell.

As I left the South Bronx today, the fierce sound of the El train initially suppressed my thinking, and soon I was being swept away in the clanging and comet-like sensations of New York's elevated train system. I was reading my daily office prayers while swaying back and forth on the train seat thinking like any adolescent male seeking a dream

156

in a book or from images of foreign places. My mission in the South Bronx was over, and I was one of the retiring, and forever changed, foreign missionary priests returning to Manhattan.

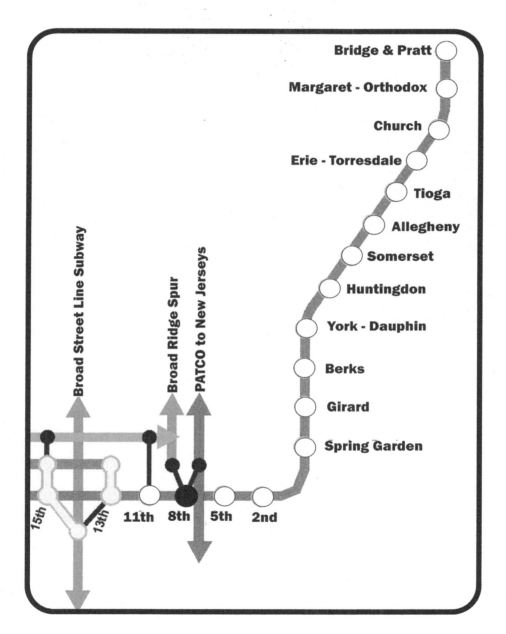

Chapter 15

The Pit

Remembering, Sounds Gentle, It's Not

I parked alongside Eckert's Meat Market and bought some chipped beef from a friendly Asian guy named, Andy. "Eckert's been gone a longtime," he said. "Retired, sold the store." The neighborhood has not attracted me for a couple years now, but I am reading Danny's stuff about life in an urban neighborhood and, well, I turned up Rising Sun off Route One and ended up standing in the Crossan Schoolyard, alone. Some curious looking maintenance guy and a tattooed woman were doing some work at the school door beside the 'Pit.'

I looked down into the pit while standing in what we thought of as center field. There was a dirty deflated rubber ball down there. I could see a guy, one of our guys, jumping the Pit fence, and landing upright, down in the pit. You couldn't see the bases from down there, but we never thought about that. You would jump in the pit, grab the ball and throw it to where you figured the base runner was.

God, I felt it, man! We all left, and it was a long time ago. I wonder what a major leaguer would think of playing center field at Crossan School.

There is nothing in the neighborhood that we are connected to except for a sense of Place. With that youth, those energies forming in specters, yet thinly visible, a thought grips, "Maybe we were all kind of stupid to leave it all behind. Think of all the people you knew back then when a walk of a couple city blocks on a summer day, or riding on a bike that same distance, prompted a hundred 'Hellos'."

I had walked the little alley from beside Eckert's to Palmetto and up to Crossan. Johnson's corner candy store is a house now with the big store windows bricked-in, no candy, no guys leaning against the walls, no school girls in colorful dresses and blouses and little kids bearing battered schoolbags and tin lunchboxes with heroes on their lids. When I looked around me in the schoolyard, dozens of people appeared. I felt the similarity to West Side Story's playground. It was us, our ghosts in tattered jeans and worn sneakers, making the dance scenes in the movie seem real, true to life.

Our old neighborhood is a very urban, citified clutch of concrete and small yards clinging to old-fashioned houses. Everything is denser than it was, crowded blocks and even its sound is off, no familiar, echoing chorus you recognized. The houses are tightly nested in a clutter of unbalanced lines like one of those celebrated but disappointing Cézanne paintings of dull village cottages, but without the landscapes. No one we knew lives there anymore.

There is a thought I have sometimes that starts out with, what if we had stayed? Like the people Danny had in his story on the North river. I'm better off staying out of the place. Let it alone, I say. Apparently, we were all prophets and knew there was no profit in staying there. It was a place of departure, maybe almost like a bus stop on a fifty-mile stretch of empty road. You had no choice.

I walked down to the hub, Five Points, and the hovel of a Bar my father practically lived in, which is all boarded up and most likely a tomb for Danny's cousin. He slept there on the pool table at times back when he was still breathing beer and whisky breaths. You couldn't play pool. Wherever he died, he never left. Maybe he is still lying on the pool table in the dust.

I am going to shake off our old neighborhood again. It is like having your ear in a shell and thinking you heard the seashore. It's only a shell and you wouldn't want to take a swim there or walk where there is nothing left. Even the walls of Crossan School are like stage settings, props that may not be used ever again, because the play doesn't run there anymore. But damn, we sure did. It was a sacrament of a place. We ardently lived and loved there and we can never forget it. Just don't go back. It doesn't exist. Besides, there is no air in the ball in the 'Pit.' No matter how good an arm you had, you could never throw a guy out with it. On top of it all, you ain't gonna find your girl, or your pals there now. Worst part, there's nobody laughing. Wherever you went, you must have got on the right bus.

Gheez!

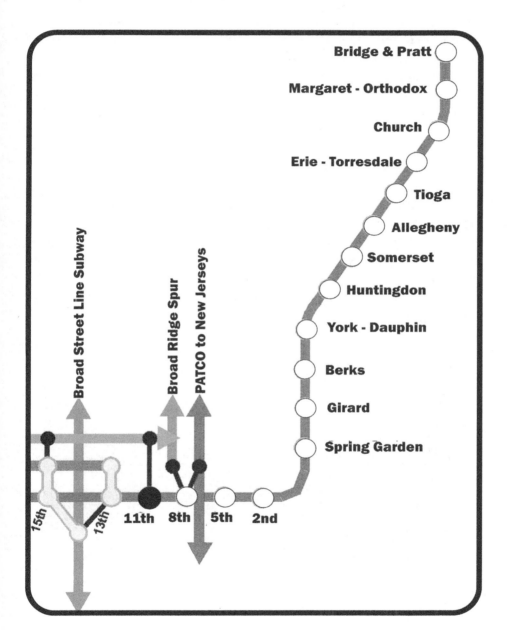

Chapter 16

As you know now, I wrote this account of Danny Fisher. The people who backed me and published this Collection on Danny asked me to tell one story about me that held what I remember most about being a kid in Philadelphia, and you know my own story. So I thought about it for a while, and not-for-nothing I rode the El train to think it over.

Somewhere past 8th Street, way into where the Philadelphia Elevated Trains went underground and turned into fast traveling, very loud subway cars. In that cacophony of exciting sounds, I thought of the Irish thing about Philadelphia.

I was a youngest son of two Irish-born parents and they were my Philadelphians. It was then all a very simple life in the working class, but filled with the wit and worth of the immigrant Irish. Our Philadelphia neighborhood was that living space we cherished where it always seemed as if only the Irish took full measure of all that surrounded them.

Here is the author's story of being an Irish American in Philadelphia:

Market-Frankford El leaving subway at Front & Arch

The Day of the Dance

In Irish America

It was a warm evening in June. Not looking back at my home, I walked slowly through the candy maker's alley and climbed over the fence to cross the Protestant churchyard. I always ran on certain forbidden shortcuts. I would never walk when I trespassed on a place. I chanted under my breath, "Top of the round ground." My mother had told me to buy that kind of meat for supper at Bruce's Butcher Shop when I got the money.

I began to breathe like an automated device until I slowed and spaced my steps across Palmetto Street to land with both feet on the loose manhole cover. As always, I sprang off it onto the curb and jumped giant steps to the taproom. Opening the door sent a shaft of embarrassing evening sunlight down the row of stools before the bar.

The linemen were perhaps the loudest and most weather-beaten of the bunch. They were roughly dressed in the brown and blue and gray 'close to the earth' colors, and all with high leather boots. They came from the big Bell Telephone garages in back of the old trolley barn. My father was one of them. I was greeted by the booming payday noise of carousing workmen and the familiar welcoming shouts; first Benny the mailman and then, from someplace near the fluorescent light that glowed over the dartboard, Clarence hollered, "Little Felix!" The roar bellowing from the workmen, plumbers, painters and the like was unceasing.

Clarence always had a Coke poured into a beer glass waiting for me. It was served at my father's usual place at the bar, beside his drinks. As was my habit, I watched the great strides of my father's sidekick. Clarence was strutting around the dart players serving loud and jovial remarks without hiding his expectation that my father, for one, would quickly join in. Surrounded by tobacco smoke, the two chums functioned within a constant volume of laughter and banter.

My father sat next to me slipping a bank teller's little brown cash envelope into my pocket. As he drank with me he spoke, briefly as usual, "Johnny, be careful with the money." Whispering in an almost reverent tone, "We'll be goin' fishin' in the morning. Do you wanna go?"

"Sure, Dad, yes!" I said.

Clarence, hearing my agreement, confirmed the plan by adding, for my father's benefit, "It'll be you, young Jonathan here, the Dutchman, big Jack Reilly and me-self."

My father tapped my chest gently, "Get the rods ready, they're in the garage, and don't forget that coffee can of sinkers we made."

The day we formed the sinkers from those Bell Telephone Company lead bars came to mind. The three of us kneeling before the blowtorch blaze, spellbound, studying the lead eggs being laid from the molten pot like secret messages to all those somber fish in the sea.

"I'll wake yuh up at five in the morning," he said gruffly. I knew his tone meant it was a promise. He raised his whiskey glass, emptied its contents in one gulp and forcefully set the glass back down on the bar. The gesture was a signal to end the arrangements and for me to be on my way.

I ran from the front door to the cement platform of the neighborhood war memorial. On the island shrine of concrete and brass, in the busy North Philadelphia intersection. I stopped to take the pay-envelope out of my pocket. I spread the money out on the steps before me. I always pretended to find it lying there. I picked it up putting a ten-dollar bill in each of my pockets. There were six of them every week. I pulled them out one at a time, as if I didn't know they were there. For a while the money was all mine. Carefully putting it back in the little envelope, I ran home without the "top of the round ground."

In my bed late that night, I heard the squeals of the front door against the weather stripping. He walked heavily into the kitchen below me. The icebox opened and closed a few times, which meant he was having what was left from supper. The stairs creaked under him and then floorboards moved loudly as he walked through the hall. Through the crack in the bathroom door, I heard the faucets gush with their full force as he made great splashing sounds against his face and gasping breaths. He always washed with the same vigor, like someone in Ireland, I imagined, at a well pump outdoors on a cold winter morning.

I climbed out of bed and found him in his room sitting on his bed, smoking in the dim light from the bathroom. He was thoughtfully removing his bandages. He wrapped his legs from rolls of slightly elastic cloth and carefully bandaged his hopelessly open sores every morning and removed them every night. He put his worst leg up, his bare foot on his bedroom chair, and turned the side of his heel up for me to examine it. He deliberately puffed his cigarette into a bright little red light and asked in a whisper, "How's it look?"

He held the cigarette glow right beside the most pus-filled sore. Stepping back into my previous place in the darkness I said, "Better," not wanting to worry him. Then I told him about the problem I'd found. "The fishing rods are all tangled from last year, Dad."

"It's all right," he said still examining his sores, "Goodnight, Johnny," his always quiet voice uttered. He spit into his palm and put the cigarette out in the spittle with the familiar hissing sound. He was kneeling at his bed blessing himself when I left the room.

=/=/=/=/=/=

It was still very quiet in the house when I saw the light from his room. He found me already getting dressed when he came to wake me. I was pleased with myself for getting up on my own. The fishing trip was beginning and I was excited and a little reckless with my noises tripping over my shoes in the dark and fumbling with a folded pant leg in the hallway. My mother and my older brothers and sisters never woke, thankfully, in spite of my falling against the hallway wall twice. Moments later we were sitting out front on the porch steps awaiting the arrival of Clarence's unmistakable black Hudson. Clarence was the only one in the world we knew who owned a Hudson automobile.

Inside the car my father and Clarence sat in the front seat talking in that subdued way they had for the time before dawn. From the back, I sat up and stared between them at the tiny yellow light in the radio.

"The Dutchman will be waiting at the apartments," Clarence said, almost singing the words.

"Big Jack's still drunk and he changed his mind about fishing, hung his head out his window and said he'd be staying there so as to die at home." They both laughed loudly. Clarence pounded the steering wheel in a rage of belly laughter and blurted out something about the Dutchman. It sent the two of them into a fit of coughing, and laughter breaking the voluntary vow of near silence they always practiced on the pre-dawn side of a fishing day. The Hudson, the shape of an inverted bathtub, pulled up a steep concrete driveway and the somber Dutchman flopped on the seat beside me without a word. We started the long ride from Philadelphia to Barnegat Bay.

Daylight broke a little more than halfway through the trip and we found ourselves on the lookout for deer. Clarence claimed we were riding on an old Indian trail. It was his way of trying to have something interesting going on for me to enjoy. I thought about the ghosts of Indians and the hidden deer around us until we left the pines and reached the small town at the bay.

We stopped under a single neon beer sign its glow dulled by the daylight. It hung over the open door of a big, wooden gray house with a taproom built into the first floor. The open door was busy airing out the stench of the previous night's activities. Within the place, some of the inside walls had been knocked out to accommodate the shoddy barroom's pool table and shuffleboard game. I saw the traces of the old walls and previous rooms marked out where different floor coverings remained. They drank their alcohol, the first of the new day, while the proprietor prepared a few bags of take-out beer. I pushed the heavy discs on the shuffleboard back and forth while waiting.

My father was telling a story about a Telephone Company employee they knew as No-Neck. "We was high up on a maintenance platform doing Penn Central's signal wiring . . . All of a sudden 'No-Neck' takes a shot of the juice; green sparks come out of his head and he burnt holes in his feet! I was holdin' him tight when he knocked us both down the ladder hole.

"Holy shit!" Clarence cried. His pleasure with the 'No-Neck' stories always showed as a red glow on his face.

"We were fallin' through the air when I figured this fat son-of-a-gun got me into another one," Clarence's eyes bulged and his mouth opened, "so I turned 'em down toward the ground and used 'em for something' soft to land on."

The bar owner said, "Damn! Was he dead, Phil?"

Well, it always seemed that 'No Neck' never died but around that time I noticed lots of people called my father Phil. My father didn't think much of his real name Felix. When asked if he had a middle name he would answer, "If I had one, do you think I'd still be using Felix?"

=/=/=/=/=/=

We drove slowly down the pebbled road from the bar and parked in a small lot near the marina. The bait house and wooden docks offered that seashore peacefulness with water splashing underneath us. We were silent, just our shoes making scuffing and thumping sounds on the dock and all the while we were wonderfully surrounded by the plangent sound of gulls and the slender terns feathering into wisps of morning fog adrift over the water.

We walked along the boat slips. One boat was sunk under the water, sitting on the bottom with a bilge pump still working and sending a string of mechanical breath to the surface. Soon we were in one of the old, unpainted, wooden rental boats. We always spent careful minutes finding the one with the least amount of water leaking into it. Clarence, at all times at the motor on the way out, was steering across the great bay to some fishing spot he had obviously decided on. His black hair, curled by the dampness of the morning, glistened above the tight wrinkles on his face.

The motor churned loud and puffed blue smoke, while the puddles of water in the bottom of the boat vibrated like jittering scenes in a faulty motion picture. Clarence squinted into the sunlight as he scanned his course. I sat in the bow with the anchor, my father and the Dutchman relaxed on the middle seat and stared sideways out across the great expanse of wind-rippled water.

I watched my father's fingers skillfully dodge the sharp old flounder hooks as he unraveled our tangled reels. The gray-white hair below his hat, like duck feathers, was the color of the sky and his eyes nearly matched the water.

I dropped my fingers into the water and watched it part. I loved the back bays. They were surrounded by marshlands and tall reed grass blowing about, giving sweeping shapes to the almost constant breezes. From our spot in the great bay, you could see a break in the land where a way to the ocean might be found. Long-necked wading birds stepped seriously about the shallow water near the sand banks. Some stood tall, white and motionless back in the grass. Now and then one would lift off and soar across the wetlands. We stopped before one of their islands.

My father used a grey stone to further sharpen the hooks and added our homemade sinkers. Clarence slapped his knees, "Here's the place, mates. The fish out here jump right in the boat, and if you're nice to 'em, they'll stay for dinner."

My father, raised up slightly, "There's something fishy about that."

The Dutchman cast first, while my father and I worked the bait on our hooks.

"Carl came to fish," my father was staring as if looking past or through us. The Dutchman nodded agreeably.

=/=/=/=/=/=

Moments later, a deep guttural sound escaped from the middle of the boat breaking another sacramental silence. It was my father. He was bending over the side of the boat twisted around and raising his outstretched lineman's boots for balance.

"Whoa! I got one!" he shouted. Then he stood slowly, reeling against the tugs and strains on his line. We all leaned toward him in empathy. The rod was taking great yanks and being forced down to the side of the boat.

"He's got two!" Clarence waved both arms and hands aloft. The brown and then white sides of the flounder flapped on the bottom of the boat between Clarence and my father. The Dutchman set his rod down carefully and grasped the line near the first fish. The flapping sounds were incredible and my father shouted, "Double header. Two hooks, two fish! Good size fish..."

"Der biting," the Dutchman said with conviction.

Clarence said, "Two beers for all hands!"

I decided to check my bait. As soon as I moved my rod, I had a bite and then a series of strong jerks. My three friends were delighted with my luck and Clarence, with his hands cupped at his mouth, yelling like a crew captain, "Pull up! Sit down! Get 'em! ... Stand up with it!"

My father quickly hung his rod on the oarlock to watch. When the fish surfaced and I lifted him out of the water he frantically fought the hook. I was helplessly off balance when I made my attempt to put him in the boat. He flapped loud against the wooden side of the boat and I fell on one knee. The fish sank into the water, still on the hook, and I felt that jerking again.

My father moaned loudly, "Good Lord! Johnny, reel 'em up." He reached out near my reel twisting his wrist around to show me what he meant. I knelt there and reeled. It worked. The fish was out of the water again. I stood up and swung it over the boat and right onto my father's legs. He slapped the fish onto the bottom of the boat. Hearing Clarence's laughter, I fell, crashing my knees into the Dutchman's back. Then the Dutchman, with bony arms, was pulling me up from his place in the boat. My father stepped on the fish and put his big hand on my shoulder, his face hidden by that big hat. He had bent his head down and when he pulled it up again you could see he was stiffened with laughter.

After they all had a can of beer, the Dutchman caught an eel that, in spite of his comical juggling, kept slipping out of his hands. With that, our luck changed. We sat in silence for about an hour waiting for more fish. Clarence mumbled something about another spot and we all reeled in for the move.

A few minutes later, Clarence shook his head looking from one side to the other. "Let's let 'er drift a bit."

My father waved to him in agreement. Clarence cut the motor and we hurried to drop the lines in again. The boat ran into a channel marker; my father pushed us away. I kept thinking I had a bite, but Clarence assured me I was feeling the sinker rubbing and bumping across the bottom.

They drank one beer after another for a while and when the drifting proved fruitless we threw the anchor over again and sat against the tide for a long time. The sun was taking its toll on us: noses, necks and hands were hot with sunburn. It was well into the afternoon. I felt a sick feeling in my stomach. I was restless and uncomfortable on the thin seat pad. My father had cleaned the flounder and flung them into a bucket of seawater in front of me. I examined them to take my mind off my increasing discomfort. I caught my father staring at me. We looked at each other for the first time that day.

"Hungry, Johnny?" He almost always used my name affectionately when he spoke to me. As soon as he said it, I realized my problem was just that.

"I'm starving, Dad."

"Here," he reached into a brown paper bag I hadn't seen and took out two sandwiches wrapped in one wrinkled clump of waxed paper. They were each made with two thick pieces of plain white bread containing a few slices of cheese, nothing else. After one bite, I knew I was going to feel a lot better. I was trying to adjust my hunger pangs to be satisfied by the sandwich, when he turned back to me and said, "Eat 'em both, Johnny, they're both yours."

"Gee, thanks, Dad. Don't you want one?"

He waved it off and turned back to his fishing. His cigarette, with a long ash, moved with his breathing. He always attracted my attention. It was, I realized later, that study of the father we all do. It concerns the father you knew and the mystery of the man you really didn't know at all. I looked at his back and the side of his face while I devoured the sandwiches. They restored my comfort and interest. The old boat seemed very cozy and the bay was friendly again.

The terns made their calls flying over us and I tried earnestly for more flounder. My father was smoking, still facing away from me. I remembered hearing him in the kitchen the night before. I thought of him making my sandwiches before going to bed. I looked at the toughened skin on his neck and then again at the shape of his back. It held a very compelling expression in its form and posture. I could never quite read that impression of him. I wondered how much of him was still the Irishman and what part now American.

=/=/=/=/=/=

171

The beer drinking, since early morning, was taking hold of their senses as it always did. We made our way back to the boat rental dock, me driving and steering the boat to the always last minute instructions of the old sailor Clarence. He would recognize channel markers and cry out their significance to me. I preferred to think of him as a seaman steeped in nautical mysteries. As always I attempted to ignore the effects of the beer.

We stopped again at the old gray house and taproom near the marina. They drank shiny brown whiskey by that point of the day and always bought the rest of the bottle in a brown bag from the bartender. The ride home began with Clarence at the wheel leading us out to the edge of the Pine Barrens.

Clarence with a Hollywood, Long John Silver expression – toughened lineman's skin and beart black around his ever-smiling lips – invited me to drive his car. When he pulled over, I got out of the Hudson and while walking behind it I looked around. The pines were lofted above the sandy soil, fallen leaves and crooked twigs.

I ended up driving the car between the edges of that green darkness while my rider's heads were bobbing in the old car. I was in that moment both twelve-years-old and more sober than I would ever notice again. For miles and miles, on both sides of the road, the dark, foreboding green trees stood at attention.

We raced along that stretch of New Jersey on an open concrete highway in total contrast to its woodland surroundings. I had to look through the steering wheel to see the wonderful road with its perfectly spaced expansion joints. My father reached up and adjusted the rear view mirror until I said I could see through it. I was able to see him in that mirror, his eyes never leaving my driving. I studied the road diligently, enjoying where the floods of sunlight seemed unable to choose between brilliant reflections or that melting like yellow butter on the roadway. Clarence coached me into higher and higher speeds. He periodically glanced back at my father a broad grin below his watery eyes.

The old car went into frightening vibrations when the harmonics of worn wheel bearings and the hopelessly unbalanced steer tires reached fifty-two miles per hour. At fifty-five those frontend mechanicals found peace again, but as Clarence warned before his face became flaccid, "too fast, the highway patrol will be on our tail."

At a steady fifty, I opened a vent window. In its welcomed sound of rushing June air, I exchanged the outside air for as much of the smell of extinguished tobacco and the fermented beer aromas as I could. I navigated the path of the car at that fast steady speed across the endless concrete expansion joints until my now noble Hudson rocked in stallion triumph from split to split and carried me in its powered rhythms through the observing pines. Soon I was gliding in the sound of the road, the tires, the friendly old motor and my own appreciation for the symphonic arrangements of it all. We sped away, while just outside the windows like silent ovations, the pines gave their windy applause.

Leaving the Barrens, the road surface changed. The sound of tires and macadam aroused Clarence. With one reddened eye opening, he searched the passing scenery for our whereabouts. He said, "Pull over, Johnny-thin." He was obviously pleased with the distance I had driven; once again he gave a Long John Silver sounding cry, "Shiver me timbers, lads, ye land lubbers," adding, "I'll take her now but young Felix here is ready to hit the bricks at the Indianapolis speedway."

The Dutchman stirred, my father not saying a word, as was his way. I pulled the car off the highway bumping a rock I couldn't even see. Clarence stepped hard on the gas pedal and the old Hudson climbed back up on the paved road. I felt betrayed by the car's indifference to the change of drivers, my recent four-wheeled companion forgetting fast our joint effort to turn ourselves into the expert equestrian and his great black steed. My mind reassembled the focused thoughts from the grand ride of the twelve-year-old. I asked some spirit of it all, how could the Hudson be held again in the grip of Clarence? My head remained filled with us prancing over the expansion joints through the sweet scent of the hosting pines.

When at last, with the Dutchman dropped off, we were home with the Hudson on the grass still clicking those heat sounds from its manifolds; my father removed the bucket with the three big flounders buried in barroom ice. He, with a stagger, took them in through the kitchen door. When he was inside the house, I could hear him asking my mother to cook them for dinner. There was always a clash with his drinking and her Irish temper. She loved fish out of the sea, however, and those who caught them were to be, at least somewhat admired, even if they were drunk. It was really a matter of how drunk.

In the dim light that fell across the yard from a neighbor's back porch, Clarence produced the wonder of wonders while seated on the kitchen steps. After maybe two or three licks from his harmonica, our backyard became the island of our amusement, and the 'Song of Clarence' became a concert. My father sang the Tipperary song and then the melancholic ballad of 'Loch Lomond.' All the music and singing was held in the June night air, wafted by the incense of smoked tobacco.

My red-haired mother was soon about her business, cooking the potatoes and the fish, the kitchen filling with the aroma of melted butter and onions and one of her breads baking in the oven. Hers was cooking of the simplest form, but performed with a drama that, I was sure, would intimidate even the grandest of chefs.

Clarence and my father wisely stayed outside the house, where the degree of their drunkenness could not be appraised or scorned by the wild Josephine. Twice she came to the kitchen door and looked out into the yard, the second time shouting out, "Sure 'n' you'll never have an hour's luck with the drink, the lot of ya."

When the hot meal was served, Clarence was welcomed into the kitchen, only because he was sober enough to perform on the harmonica. Seated next to me, he filled a shot glass with beer, which he hid for me behind the jars of jam. My mother ate her fish, the one I caught, to the bone. When she got up, gathering the plates, Clarence fled back outside. Soon the harmonica sent its music, a spirited reel, back into her kitchen. She smiled broadly and set the dishes down. Tilting her head and lifting her knee in rocking repetition, she was soon twirling in a jig she called "Shoe the Donkey." My father, first just sanding cautiously in the open doorway, stepped inside the kitchen and sat at his chair. He clapped and bellowed unintelligible but rhythmic lyrics, while I, taking advantage of the commotion and hidden behind his large form, drank my tiny glass of beer. After a few rollicking moments, the music ended, and – as suddenly as if a curtain had fallen – she retreated into her sewing room, where we all knew she hid a bottle of red wine under a dresser. She stayed there, the old Singer sewing machine spinning its own rapid ovations, and her smoking her Old Gold cigarettes, until my brothers and sisters returned from their day.

Somewhere in that time, the black Hudson would reverse off the grass and down the driveway where it would turn about under the street light and be gone. My father would go back up to his bed, remove his bandages, extinguish a cigarette in the spittle in his palm and snore loud behind a closed door.

=/=/=/=/=/=

As for me, I remember gong tip-toe to the back door and sitting on the kitchen steps in the dark smoking one of my father's cigarettes. The day lingered in the pleasure of my tobacco. Being twelve was the best time in my childhood because I lived in a special solitude between the worlds around me, visited only by the best they had to offer yet unaffected, in any conscious way, by the worst.

I was still young when I left home. I remember my father spoke his good-byes to me while sitting on a stack of Bell Telephone pole cross members he and Clarence had borrowed, as they said, and piled behind the old garage. I went back years later when he was dying and I cared for him, feeding him simple meals and shaving his old, stubby whiskers.

I bathed him, washing his back, white and bony and bent with age. Near the end, I told him how I felt about him while he was looking right at me. He whispered about Ireland and about the fishing, became silent, as was his way, and died in the morning.

Clarence and I carried him. Clarence, a step ahead of me, was old, quiet and sober. The wrinkles on his face were permanent, his hair stiff looking and gray. He slipped out of the graveyard and disappeared down through two long rows of silent pine trees. I have never seen him since, except maybe when I see a stretch of bay water or an old boat or flounder lying brown, flat, and still, on the ice in a fish store.

I know now that I had everything I needed when I was twelve, and I remember it all. Yes, my father comes back to me in that familiar and quiet awareness he showed me of those simple things – like two good sandwiches and when men talk of fishing or someone asks if I want cheese on my sandwich.

56 Trolley under El going west
on Torresdale Avenue

Live under the Market-Frankford El circa 1976

Epilogue

My Biography or "You'se Guys Need My Street Creds?"

I've been thinking of how we even speak Philadelphian, for example, how we say "You'se Guys," our plural for "you." I believe I can write Philadelphia-based stories, but you gotta be given my credentials. So here ya go...

Football in the City 1950's Author #24, Danny Fisher is #3 our Quarterback

Between being born and raised in a neighborhood, playing football and hose ball on the streets between parked cars, and then playing football in Municipal Stadium with my name called out on the loud speaker for a tackle when I was twelve. Flicking bottle caps in the school yard, Knowing how to cross the city on one bus fare, thinking that elevated trains and subways were as fast as comets, working the Docks for years where the sound of a ship's fog horn was a match for any cry in the wilderness, earning a third of my living at the food center in South Philly where a hand shake was as good as any paper, and dodging the wanna-be gangsters was part of the scene – and my memories, I find are many.

I will always remember playing in a String Band that won First Prize at City Hall twice, trying to swim the Delaware River, being in a Street Gang at fifteen, running from the cops on summer nights with thirty

Shooting Broad Street from South Philly 1977, You'se Guys tripping the light fantastic, Author left side banjo

177

Da other guys -
and the way we were then.
Call 'em all You'se Guys

guys meeting-up later on the roof of Jardel Recreation center, hanging on truck and car bumpers when it snowed, dying of laughter over what happens hanging on a corner, hearing rock–n-roll music like it was as sacred as the hymns the Nuns beat into us.

Nicknames were more meaningful than your Christian name; mine was simply, Muc, or more often, Jimmy Dean. Then there was Pop Warner football and proudly wearing the gold and black uniform while walking across the neighborhood for a Sunday afternoon game. Five Points Tavern was written on the back of my baseball team shirt. Being kicked out of Connie Mack Stadium and sneaking back in. Sledding at Burholme Park until you were so wet and cold even you had to stop and anyway your dog was freezing. Waiting in the lines around the block to get into the Oxford Movies,

Being taken to the roof of the Philadelphia Art Museum to write about the place, drinking Iron City beer in brown bags after a great game of softball in our part of Fairmount Park with both the older gang "The Counts" and my gang, "The Streakers." knowing people of every nationality on the globe, signing up for the Army at 401 North Broad Street, nearly drowning in the Schukle (and not knowing how to spell it), Maybe I'm proud about winning a short story contest, first prize for excellence, about Philadelphia that exposed the cold rejection of young black musicians by some jerks that were still influential in Philly's 100 year-old Mummers parade.

Being in the first graduating class at CD High, Going to Temple University by hitchhiking down 9th Street because I didn't have the money for the Subway or books for that matter, and then a Community College degree after ten years of night school, and many years of classes at U. Penn where I have been the oldest and dumbest kid in class, but got a short story published, and was a member of the Class of 2015 graduating at age 73.

Then there's, marrying "The Girl from G Street" I always met at the K & A Elevated Stop or 30th Street Station after work, "The Girl" from Kensington. I got issued a girl from Little Flower High School who grew up in a row house on a street so narrow that only one car fits out front while in the back was an alley that took raw courage to trespass. The proposal was in the school yard at G and Westmoreland and it has stuck for fifty-two years.

The Author and the Girl from G Street.

Author Biography

John A. McCabe, a lifelong writer in all genres, is an active member of the Writers Guild at the Pearl S. Buck Writing Center. His novel, *The Grey Pennies*, centers on his studies of Hiroshima and Nagasaki. A short story writer, he has authored two short story collections. *Tracks Through Our Lives: Stories Told on the Philly El Trains* recounts Philadelphia stories and tales of remarkable friendships. His second short story collection, *The Bridge Walker*, consists of seventy titles.

McCabe was published by the National Society of Collegiate Scholars 2010 as a University of Pennsylvania Chapter participant with *The Wedding Guests*. His works appear in the online PSB Literary Journal. He has also published poetry. John was a recent Presenter at the West Virginia University Gateway Conference honoring the legacy of Pearl S. Buck. His topic was Pearl's 1959 novel, *Command the Morning*, her historic fiction exposé of the Manhattan Project.

McCabe's novel The Grey Pennies highlights the story of two Philadelphian U.S. Soldiers subjected to atomic bomb testing involving charging troops on ground zero. The haunting novel evokes the memory of Hiroshima and Nagasaki.

Being irradiated in the 4th Infantry in 1962.
Author - the guy breaking ranks on the right.

Made in the USA
Monee, IL
09 February 2021